CATHRYN PETIT

Soars My Heart, Soft as Silk

I ♥ Y Green
Publishing, LLC

For my love, Charlie. Dance with me for as long as the music plays.

Contents

Acknowledgement

Illustrations: To my talented daughter-in-law, Tori Uncapher, whose artful handwriting and sketches brought Lucia's letters to life.

Edits: To troupe leader extraordinaire and fellow bellydancer, Angela Petry, for her masterful edits of Book 3 and for her talented audio productions of the Sisters of the Silk Veil series.

Prologue: September 2019

Golden rays streamed through the twenty-foot wall of windows, spotlighting the tiny feet and giant paws that pattered the tiled floors. The vibrancy of this house was such a far cry from the dull Washington apartment from another lifetime ago.

She hadn't even minded giving up her little yellow rental. She had lived in the quaint downtown house from the time she moved to Southbridge until the day they all moved into this grand family home ten months earlier.

Lydia howled hysterically at the erupting commotion.

"Mom, don't just stand there. Do something."

Lydia mustered enough composure to snag Romeo's collar. "Sit."

He obeyed, but his head snapped from side to side watching the little ones fly by.

Johnathan was loudly protesting the costumes draped over Jewell's arms as Olivia followed behind on wobbly toddler legs.

"They're just for Halloween," Jewell called above the ruckus.

"You're not getting me into sissy clothes." Johnathan flailed his arms.

Jewell plopped onto the sofa and pretended to cry into cupped hands.

"Mommy, don't cry." The two children rushed to her side.

"Gotcha!" She laughed and flung them onto the sofa. Lydia and Romeo jumped in.

"Now what's wrong with these costumes?"

"They're for girls." Johnathan folded his arms and frowned.

"No, Mommy has a friend who's coming to visit us next month. He's a bellydancer and performs in restaurants wearing costumes just like this one." She held up the harem pants and choli top for emphasis. "Wait until you meet him. You'll want to wear the costume then. Now, can we try them on?"

"Yay!" Olivia bounced with excitement, clapping her tiny hands.

"No." Johnathan shook his head.

"Okay, I can wait until you meet Andrea. Maybe you'll change your mind then. If not, Mommy will get you whatever costume you want."

"A pirate!"

"Arg." Lydia winked.

"Deal," Jewell said.

She turned her focus to Olivia and guided the little one to stand in front of her as she pulled the pink bellydance skirt over her head and down over the top of her shorts. She then replaced the unicorn T-shirt with the costume's cropped top. She positioned the silver headband on top of Olivia's head. Jewell looked adoringly at how the silver accented the baby girl's soft black curls. Her heart filled with love.

Satisfied with her cuteness, she turned to share the moment with Lydia, who sniffed back tears. Jewell slid closer to her mother to place an arm around her.

Three sharp clacks of the door knocker interrupted their family time. Lydia looked as bewildered as Jewell.

Jewell crossed the living room to the foyer. She ascended the tiled platform to the double doors. When she peeked through the peephole, there stood a supermodel-looking woman, poised to drop the knocker again.

One

Chapter 1: Labor Day 2018, One Year Earlier

J ewell and Lydia returned home from the hot-air balloon festival. "What a great day." Lydia thrust her hands to the ceiling for a big stretch.

"It was. Do you want some tea, I'm going for a glass of wine." Jewell slid the scrunchie from her ponytail and shook loose her long blonde spirals.

"Actually, I'm pretty wiped out. I think I'll head to bed."

Jewell felt too wide awake and invigorated to go to bed. She was still reeling from the success of the chance encounter she and Christian had staged for Jewell to meet Johnathan on the sly. She understood his caution in introducing his young son to the women he dated.

Jewell grabbed a glass of wine and positioned herself in front of the computer. She peeked around the corner to verify Lydia was out of sight. A few pecks on the keyboard and she was back where she had left off. Her secret search. She rolled the mouse, then jolted from the shock as she landed on a photo of Nathanael as a car salesman under

1

the name "Nate Miles." The advertisement documented the location as a mountainous Tennessee town southeast of Nashville.

Nathanael's blatant public profile baffled her. It didn't jive with the activities of someone in a witness protection program. That had been her only theory about her brother when he not only disappeared from the correctional system a year earlier, but had also mysteriously vanished from the face of the earth. She figured he had provided evidence to implicate members of the crime ring and in turn required protection.

She searched further and saw a wedding announcement. The caption below the picture read, "Nate and Breanna Miles." Hmm, she had a sister-in-law. By the date, December 1, 2017, she realized they must have gotten married soon after he had moved. She scrolled through more searches until a tragic headline blasted the screen and paralyzed her.

Shaken and unsure of how to handle the news, she texted Becca.

I know it's late. Can we meet? Early in the morning before you go to class? I have something major to discuss.

Sure. What is it?

Let's talk in the morning.

R U okay?

I am. Talk to you in the morning. Rhita's 7 a.m.?

K.

Jewell found Becca waiting for her in front of Rhita's. It comforted her to see her best friend wearing a sunny smile and waving enthusiastically. Before her move to Southbridge, Jewell's only other true friend had been Josh. Josh, with his strong teddy bear hugs and steadfast love.

The thought of his untimely death still haunted her.

"Hey chica, what's up?" Becca moved towards Jewell. "Uh-oh, you don't look happy. Is it Christian?"

"No, it's something beyond belief. C'mon, let's go in." She took Becca's arm as they entered Rhita's.

"Want your usual?"

"No, I don't think I could keep anything down."

"Oh, no, it is bad. I'll just get a coffee to-go later. They won't mind us sitting here."

Jewell spotted a free table for two next to the window and nodded toward it. The pair made their way past the patrons to the more secluded table.

Becca hung her backpack over the chair and situated herself to face Jewell, leaning forward as if to focus.

Jewell sat opposite and placed her feet on the chair rung. She held her cell phone in her right hand and folded her arms tight across her abdomen.

"You're pale." Becca leaned in closer and squinted.

"I didn't sleep a wink. You won't believe this." Jewell took a deep breath and slowly blew it out. "I secretly searched for Nathanael. For Mom's sake."

"Why on earth did you start that? We'll have to deal with him now if you find him."

"No. No worries there."

Jewell unfolded her arms, swiped the screen of her phone and with trembling hands, slid it to Becca.

Becca stared at the screen. She covered her mouth, shaking her head as tears formed. She slid the phone back to Jewell who read the headline again, *Gang Guns Down Young Couple in Broad Daylight.*

Through tears, Jewell explained how on July third, someone apparently killed Nathanael and his wife in a drive-by shooting on a major public sidewalk.

"Only two months ago." Becca stretched out a chunk of her brunette strands and vigorously twirled them.

"It appears someone or some group specifically targeted them. The article says she was the daughter of Sarah and Edward Moore from the same town. No mention of Nate Miles' family, of course."

"That's so sad."

"I wonder why Nathanael got so careless?" Jewell looked to the ceiling. "Why would he have taken on such a public profile? He should have been in witness protection."

"Really? Ah!" Becca hit her forehead with the heel of her hand, then reached for Jewell. "I am so sorry I said anything negative. I never dreamed…"

"I know, neither did I. Nathanael had gotten away with everything his whole life. He was so tough. I honestly thought he was invincible."

"But, witness protection?" Becca tilted her head.

"That's all I could figure. I was still tracking him, you know, thanks to his blackmailing escapade. The last record I had was of him in the Port Eastland jail last September. Then nothing. Ha, I had no desire to search for him then. I was grateful to have him tucked away somewhere. That was until Mom came into my life."

"What do you think happened?"

"I'm guessing this gang sought him out. I can't imagine it was random, given his circumstances. But if he was in witness protection, he shouldn't have been in an advertisement as a car salesman or have a wedding announcement in the newspaper. I just can't figure it out."

"Aw, you had a sister-in-law. It's hard to imagine him married."

"Yeah, she was pretty. About our age. I'll show you the wedding announcement sometime."

"It's just awful," Becca said. "I mean, not knowing anything about him or his location was okay with me. I rarely thought about him, but this…gosh, now I'd welcome the sight of him across the street leaning against the tavern."

"Ha! Go figure, me too. Now, how do I tell Mom?"

"Oh, no. Lydia!" Becca closed her eyes and shook her head. "I'll go with you."

"But what about your classes?" Jewell asked.

"I think I can miss class for something like this."

Becca and Jewell left Rhita's and trekked to the little yellow house. Jewell loved her quaint little downtown rental. She found it online and had been enjoying it for over a year now, ever since her cross-country journey from Washington. She loved the airy whimsy of the blue and white interior with its mermaid decor.

They found Lydia at the kitchen island drinking her morning coffee.

"Where did you get off to so early? I was going to make breakfast but saw your bedroom door open and you gone. And why aren't you in class, Becca?"

"I needed to talk to Becca about something this morning."

"Oh?" Lydia asked, then cocked her head, studying the pair. "Jewell, something's wrong. Are you okay? Everything seemed fine when I went to bed last night. Did something happen between you and Christian?"

"No." Jewell shook her head and wondered why everyone's first thoughts went to Christian.

Jewell and Becca joined Lydia at the island.

Lydia swiveled on her stool to stand. "Coffee?"

"No, Mom, please stay where you are. I have something to tell you."

"Oh?"

"Yes, I was, um…I mean I had started…well, as a favor to you…"

"Yes? Go on."

"I was searching for Nathanael."

"You were?" Lydia straightened on the stool and smiled. "I'm surprised."

"Well, I tracked him to a town in Tennessee."

"That's great. Let's go get him."

"I wish we could," Jewell said, then glanced toward Becca for support. "You have no idea how much I wish we could. But we can't. Not any longer."

"Of course we can. Everyone will make up. You'll see. Things have a way of sorting themselves out. Look at the two of us."

Jewell turned to Becca, then inhaled deeply. She stood and went to Lydia's side.

"Mom, I have awful news."

"What?" Lydia crossed her arms over her chest and stared intently at Jewell.

"Ugh, there's no other way than to just say it. I'm sorry. But Nathanael was killed. Shot. Probably by the gang he had gotten tangled with."

"What? When?" Lydia's voice escalated.

"July third. This year."

Lydia sat staring at Jewell for what she knew was only moments but felt like hours. Then she turned to Becca, who had tears streaming from her eyes. Lydia stood and smoothed her summer dress over her long lean body. "I will lie down for a while."

"Mom."

Becca shook her head. Jewell caught Becca's message and didn't chase after her.

Lydia headed to her room, and Jewell flinched at the sound of the door slamming behind her.

"What now?" she asked Becca.

"You let her grieve however she needs to. Just be here. Don't leave her alone."

"I won't. Of course not." She shook her head. "I guess it's a good thing I didn't go back to my old job."

"Agreed," Becca said.

"Why don't you go ahead and get to your class."

"Are you sure?"

"I'm sure. We'll be fine. Besides, you're turning out to be quite the psychologist and I think I'll need your expertise."

"Okay." Becca smiled. "But I'll stop by after my shift at the bookstore."

Days passed with Lydia self-confined in her bedroom. Jewell didn't leave the house. Troupe members stopped by daily. Sometimes alone, sometimes in pairs. Christian spent every evening with Jewell. He explained how he had arranged for either the nanny or his folks to stay with Johnathan and planned to continue every evening for as long as Jewell and Lydia needed.

Each evening, Christian either brought enough takeout for the three of them or reheated meals the troupe members had dropped off. And each evening, full of hope, Jewell carried out the ritual of fixing a plate for Lydia, arranging it on a tray with a drink and a flower plucked from the flower bed Lydia had planted. Then later each evening, Jewell returned defeated with a practically untouched tray.

The only time Lydia surfaced was for a trip to the bathroom they shared in between their bedrooms. Jewell held her breath each time Lydia emerged, hoping she was coming to join them in the living room. But each time, she returned to her room and closed the door.

"Is she at least drinking?" he asked.

"Yes. Tea and juice. And picking at the food."

"Well, at least that's something."

These long evenings provided Jewell and Christian with some intense alone time. They played music, keeping it low enough to hear Lydia should she call for them. She never did. They took turns discussing their lives and ran the gamut from their first memories all the way to the present day.

"Say, do you want to play chess?" Jewell stood and walked to the entertainment center, not waiting for his answer. "I've got a set in here somewhere...ah-ha!" She located and snatched the box.

She made her way back to Christian, box in hand, waggling her eyebrows.

"Sure, I'm game if you don't mind losing." Christian blew on his fingernails and brushed them against his shirt.

"Ha. We'll see."

Jewell set the black and white board on the cafe table at the edge of the kitchen island. Her chessboard was smooth and shiny with corresponding alabaster pieces. "I get white," Jewell said, "because I'm pure."

Christian's eyes narrowed and his mouth twisted.

Jewell arranged her pieces and watched as Christian stretched his arms out and melodramatically flexed his fingers then placed his left hand on his right shoulder and swung that arm in wide erratic circles.

With her index finger tapping the corner of her lip, she acknowledged him. "Really?"

"What? Am I psyching you out?"

"Hardly."

They shared a laugh and started out with dueling pawn moves.

"Jewell?"

"Oh sure, wait until I have my hand on my knight."

"No, I was just going to...never mind, go ahead and make your lame knight move."

"Lame knight move, huh?"

"Yikes. No, not bad actually. Well, what I was going to ask you." Christian studied the board. "You said when you were under anesthesia and had that...that...I hate to even say the words."

"Near-death experience?" Jewell helped him out.

"Yeah." Christian moved his knight. "You said you believe you saw Josh in heaven. So I was wondering what faith you are, where you go to church?"

"Church?" Jewell asked. "Oh, I don't. Never really have. None of my foster parents took me. Josh's grandmother never took him. So we really weren't churchgoers. Why?" She castled her king.

"Uh-oh, I see my warmup did nothing to prepare me for playing against you." Christian chuckled.

Jewell blew on her fingernails and rubbed them on her shirt.

"I was just asking because I go. My folks and Johnathan and I." He squinted at the chessboard.

"Where?"

"The Methodist. Here in town."

"Do you want me to go too?"

"Completely up to you."

They continued to play and enjoy the background music. Jewell had set her music on Alexa to shuffle stations.

"Hey, I love that song," Jewell said.

"Well, ma'am, it's mighty countrified."

"It is."

Christian stood and progressed toward Jewell, his face adorned with his widest grin. The sparkle in his green eyes and the dark loops of his hair melted her. She was even growing accustomed to his British accent, and it provided her with plenty of teasing opportunities. Arm stretched out and palm turned up, he reached for her.

9

She flushed, her eyes snapped to the floor then back to his as an impromptu smile tightened her cheeks. She took hold of her wrap skirt and twisted her legs to face him. She gently placed her hand in his.

"May I have this dance?"

She nodded and stood as he pulled her into him, pushing out a giggle.

"Do you two-step?"

She shook her head.

Christian positioned himself in front of her. His right arm around her tiny waist and her right hand lightly in his left. He pulled their linked hands up and to the side in a closed dance position.

"Okay, on the count of three, step back on your right foot then back on your left foot. Then keep repeating."

She followed his instructions as he moved forward on the opposite foot. They repeated the process a couple of times, traveling in a circle around the kitchen floor.

"This is it?" She asked. "This is just walking."

"Ah, you think so? Now we'll keep this up, but to the counts of quick-quick, slow-slow."

"A-ha, a little trickier." She giggled as she tried to keep up with his counts, sometimes jamming things up by going slow to his quick.

Once they fell into a rhythm, another great country song played and he began twirling her as they circled the kitchen. Jewell's spins grew wider and faster as she got the hang of it, her smile so big her cheeks ached.

Christian began changing positions by bringing Jewell to his side so they both danced forward in promenade fashion. She became playful in the dance, interjecting bellydance undulations and twists. They cackled.

When the song ended, she wrapped her arms around him roaring in laughter as he lifted her from her feet and spun her off the ground.

Tears of joy moistened the corners of her eyes.

When it was time for Christian to leave that evening, they lingered longer in their goodnight kiss.

On the sixth evening, as Jewell and Christian settled into their new routine, Lydia appeared through the doorway. Jewell leaped to her feet and nervously surveyed her every move. Romeo ran to Lydia, whining and wagging his entire body with his tail. She knelt next to him and buried her face in his black standard poodle curls.

"I know," she said to him. "I went away. But I'm back." She stood and Jewell rushed to her side.

"I'm glad you're back. You must be hungry?"

"Starved actually." A weak smile sneaked over her face. "Hi, Christian."

"Hi, Lydia." Christian stood. "You two sit. Let me heat something up."

"Thank you, Christian. I'll eat something light and then I need to go to one of my AA meetings. I already texted Sherry."

"You did?" Jewell felt a sting. But, she knew Sherry and Lydia shared a bond she would never fully understand and she was grateful Lydia had the support.

"Yes, I don't need a repeat of the downward spiral like the last time I grieved. God knows I wrecked a whole lot of people's lives." She squeezed Jewell's arm.

Christian and Jewell hung around the living room awaiting Lydia's return. When she arrived home from the AA meeting she passed Maya, scooped her up and sat on the chair next to the sofa where Jewell and Christian sat.

"I haven't seen you for some time," she said, stroking the calico cat. "Jewell?"

"Yes."

"Tell me everything you discovered about Nathanael."

"Well, he lived in a small town southeast of Nashville. It's in the mountains. He was a car salesman. Do you want to see?"

"Yes. I think I do."

Christian squeezed Jewell's hand. She stood and made her way to the computer with Lydia following.

"You sit here." Jewell pulled out the office chair for her then knelt on the floor next to it. She maneuvered the keyboard and mouse so she could operate them from her position. Christian stood behind Lydia's chair.

She scrolled to the dealership advertisement with her ruggedly good looking brother standing next to a new car. Lydia placed her hand over her mouth and inhaled sharp and deep through her nose.

Lydia's hand shook as she removed it to say, "Look how handsome." She touched the screen.

"Yep, he had no problems in that department."

Then she showed her the wedding announcement.

"How sweet." Lydia began to smile, then dropped her head and frowned. "I had a daughter-in-law."

Jewell looked to Christian, and he shrugged, his expression grave.

"Do you want to see anything else?" Jewell asked, gingerly.

"No, I'm good."

Jewell's shoulders slumped in relief. The last thing she wanted was to show Lydia the article about the shooting.

"The wedding announcement mentioned her parents were local to that area."

"Yes, I saw that too."

"Let's find them."

"You want to find her parents?"

"Of course. Wouldn't you? I want to learn as much as I can about him and his life up until…well, up until then."

"Okay," Jewell said, again glancing to Christian.

"Then, that's exactly what we'll do," Christian said. "Take a trip. How about next weekend?"

Jewell stood to throw her arms around him. "That works for me." Then she whispered in his ear, "Thank you."

"It works for me too," Lydia said. "Now I'm exhausted and heading for bed."

"Okay, Mom. Do you want a snack?"

"No, I think I'm caught up for now. I'll make breakfast in the morning. Time to get back to normal."

They said their goodnights to Lydia and returned to the sofa. Christian moved closer to Jewell and placed his arm around her shoulders. She luxuriated in the sensation as every muscle warmed and relaxed under his touch. She marveled at how familiar he felt so early in their relationship as she snuggled in under his strong arm.

"I guess we can resume dating," he said. "Don't get me wrong, spending time here and learning about your life has been perfect, but I'd fancy a little romance and going out into the real world."

"Agreed." Jewell drew her knees up and over his thighs. "But these last few nights haven't exactly been unromantic."

They kissed a lover's kiss. Jewell thrilled at the dizzying waves washing over her.

"I've got to get back to Johnathan."

"Aw, I understand. Will he come with us next weekend?"

"I don't think so. Emotions may be raw. My folks can come to the house and stay with him."

They meandered to Jewell's front door, her hand in his with fingers intertwined like a growing vine. He leaned down and kissed her again, then took her other hand, holding her gaze.

Jewell sighed, and he broke away.

As if coming out of a daze, Christian spoke. "We need to plan our trip. I'll drive."

Jewell nodded, then watched as he turned and made his way down the sidewalk to his car.

"Thanks for going with us," she called to him.

"Absolutely. That's what people do." He turned back to flash her his impossibly bright smile.

Jewell summoned Romeo and headed out for their nightly walk, all the while deeply engrossed in thoughts of Christian. So much so that for a moment she nearly forgot about Nathanael and his bride's tragic end. That was until she returned home and passed Lydia's room.

"Jewell?"

"Oh, you're up."

"Can you come in?"

Jewell entered Lydia's room and sat on the bed. Lydia moved toward the middle to make room for her. Time passed as they lay in silence.

"How was it when you lost Josh? Do you remember?"

"Sure, I remember. As if it was yesterday, sometimes." Jewell took Lydia's hand in hers, then rolled onto her back, staring at the white ceiling.

"Yeah. It's been twenty-six years since your father was killed in the accident, but I still remember it like it was yesterday. Isn't it funny how that is? It must have been traumatic for you—finding Josh."

"It was. When I saw him, lying there on the rug, it felt like I didn't have anyone." She stopped and remembered Nathanael's involvement and how he was more concerned about his own welfare and escaping the police than Josh's death and Jewell's loss. She forced herself to stop that train of thinking before reaching the blackmail part. There was no value in resentment. Both Josh and Nathanael were gone now.

"I felt like I didn't have anyone, but when I came back, Becca, the troupe and Kage were all here for me, I just didn't see it. I fell into a black hole. The hole is still there, right smack in the middle of my chest." She paused. "Only, it's as if gardens have grown around the hole covering it to prevent me from falling through. Gardens planted, watered and tended by my friends and…and now, by you and Christian. I think of it like those sites on the road. You know, spots where accidents occurred, where people drop off crosses with flowers and cards and stuffed animals. My friends, you and Christian, drop those things off daily for me."

A soft hush hung in the room as they continued to lay still.

Jewell broke the quiet. "You know I'm here. And all my friends. And your friends. You've gotten close to Della Rae and Lynn. Oh, plus you and Sherry have that whole thing."

"I know. I do have a lot of people who care about me."

"It's just…I guess what I'm saying," Jewell continued, "I don't want you to slip into any black holes. There's no need to. It seems, from your stories, you were alone when Dad died. You're far from being alone now."

"Hmm, you're right. I was alone, more or less back then. And you're pretty smart. I mean I know you're a genius when it comes to higher learning, but I think you're doing pretty well with life's lessons as well. I think more than you realize. Back to your dad and when he died. The grief itself was horrendous enough, but all the complications that ensued afterward were the killer for me."

"It sounds like it. Do you want to talk about it?"

Jewell heard soft snores coming from Lydia. She eased her hand loose, pulled the covers over Lydia's shoulders, then left for her own room.

Two

Chapter 2

The next morning Jewell awoke to the smell of bacon frying. She sat up in bed and to no surprise, found Romeo sniffing in the savory scent from underneath the door.

"She's driving you crazy too, huh? Let's go." Jewell got out of bed, slid into her slippers and made her way to the kitchen with Romeo bounding ahead.

"Morning," Jewell said as Lydia was about to smack an egg on the edge of a skillet.

"Morning, you two."

"How are you?" Jewell asked as she reached her hands toward the ceiling for a big stretch.

"I feel like it's a fresh day. That's how I feel."

"It is. And I'm especially glad to hear you say so."

"I'm looking forward to our trip next weekend."

"Me too, we need to plan with Christian."

"He's a good person, Jewell."

"Yes, he really is." Jewell smiled.

"I think he grounds you." Lydia skillfully flipped an egg.

"Is that what I'm feeling? You know, I don't like to compare, but I guess it's human nature. He seems to have the perfect combination of grounding me like Josh did and then like Kage, he, well…" Jewell's eyes moved from side to side as she searched for the right words to use with her mother.

"Turns you on?" Lydia asked.

"Um, yeah. Turns me on." She laughed.

"Well, then, that's the perfect combination." With spatula still in hand, Lydia moved toward Jewell and bumped hips.

Jewell giggled and her cheeks flushed.

"By the way, I found our wayward cat and fed her," Lydia said.

"Yeah, she's unpredictable."

"Grab some plates. This is about ready."

Jewell retrieved two plates from the cabinet and laid them on the counter next to the stove. She hadn't imagined this tiny kitchen so active with cooking and baking when she first moved into her rental.

They were in the middle of eating breakfast with Romeo at his bowl, lapping up his rationing of bacon crumbled over his food, when Christian called.

"Is this too early?" he asked. "I know it was late when you texted your zzz's emoji last night."

"No, it's good. We're eating, but it's okay."

"I'll call back. I have an update about the trip."

"No, really go ahead. Mom's here, so let me put you on speaker. We can eat while you talk."

Jewell laid the phone on the counter and pushed the speaker icon.

"Hi, Lydia."

"Hi, Christian. Thank you for doing this."

"It's my pleasure. So, I spoke to my folks and they can come to stay with Johnathan Saturday morning through Sunday evening."

"That's great," Lydia said.

"I know you're the Internet explorer, Jewell, but I found a cute motel. It's right in town. I secured two rooms side by side; one for you and Lydia and one for me."

Lydia threw a smirk in Jewell's direction.

"I hope it's okay that I already rented them. I can cancel if need be."

"No, they sound great." Jewell tilted her head, returning Lydia's smirk.

"Oh, and Jewell, I made sure it's pet friendly."

"That's great for future reference, but I think I'll get Becca to check in on him and Maya this trip. There won't be much outdoor time for him. At least not this trip."

"Whatever you think's best. The rest of the work is up to you, Jewell, in locating Breanna's parents and arranging a meeting."

"Done," Jewell said.

Lydia dropped her fork.

"What? When?" Christian asked.

"At least the locating them part, that is. How long did you two expect it to take me? Honestly. Now, I just need to call and try not to shock or upset them."

"Maybe I'd better call them," Lydia said.

"That would make me feel better," Jewell said.

"Okay," Christian continued. "What I was thinking was, I could pick you both up Saturday morning. It's a good eight-hour drive. We'll stop along the way for lunch, so figure at least nine hours altogether. If that doesn't work for them, or if they don't want us to visit, let me know."

"Sounds like a plan," Jewell agreed. "We're on it. Wish us luck."

"Always. Talk to you later. Bye, Lydia."

Jewell disconnected the call as she finished her toast and bacon, but pushed the plate with the cold egg aside.

Lydia stood to gather the dishes. "You need to get to your bellydance class this week too. I hate you missed last week."

"It's okay." Jewell gathered her plate and mug. "Here, I'll help."

They cleaned up the kitchen. Lydia gathered her AA book with her scratched notes sticking out here and there and left to meet Sherry at their usual time.

Later that day, Lydia's sweet voice rang from the patio, but Jewell couldn't quite make out her words. She had stepped out onto the patio with her cell phone after Jewell handed her a scrap of paper with the Moore's phone number on it.

Jewell was reaching for some cookies when she heard Lydia slide the patio door open and reenter the house.

"They agreed with our plans. You can let Christian know the trip is a go. They'll be expecting us around three or so."

"Wow. How'd they react to your phone call?"

"Mr. Moore answered, but was struggling to hear me. I've been told I have a soft voice."

"You do."

"Well, he put Mrs. Moore on the phone. She gasped when I explained who I was. But then we talked for a bit and she seemed to process the information. Said they would love to meet us and our plans were fine. They're both retired."

"Okay, great. I'll let Christian know."

"Oh, Mrs. Moore said to call her Sadie."

That Saturday, Christian arrived at 7 a.m.

"You gals ready to roll?" He asked as Jewell opened the front door.

"We are," Lydia called from the kitchen.

"What's that incredible smell?"

Jewell motioned toward the kitchen. "Mom got up early and baked cinnamon rolls."

"That's it!" Christian joked. "Lydia, I'm putting you in my will."

"It's no big deal," she said. "It's not like I was going to sleep anyway."

"Nervous?" He asked as he reached to help with their luggage.

"A little."

Jewell explained to Romeo and Maya that they would return and she would bring them each a treat. Romeo cocked his head and whined.

The three hit the sidewalk, making their way to Christian's car. Jewell carried her overnight bag, Lydia wheeled her small suitcase, and Christian carried Lydia's cosmetic bag and the sweet-smelling baked goods.

"Do you think I overdressed?" Lydia asked, turning to Jewell. She wore a casual maxi-length skirt, sea foam in color, and an off-white lace top. Colorful jewels adorned her sandal straps. She had styled her long black hair into a casual bun with the perfect amount of loose strands dangling about her silver hooped earrings. A silver chain around her neck complemented the hoops.

"No, I think you look perfect. Maybe I'm under dressed?" She examined her khaki shorts and floral top and noticed Christian matched her look with his own khaki shorts and a blue T-shirt. Jewell did, however, take the time to fuss her blonde curls into a half-updo and to apply her favorite chalk pink lipstick. Plus, she had carefully selected her pink statement sunglasses to pick up the color in her floral top.

Christian opened the trunk of his 1971 Mercedes. As he arranged their belongings, he eased their wardrobe doubts by assuring them he would be the envy of every eye when they entered the restaurant for lunch.

The recorded voice of the GPS spouted, "Turn left, and in 500 feet, your destination will be on the right."

Jewell heard Lydia draw in a deep breath from the back seat. She reached to take her hand.

"You'll be fine. We're with you," Jewell assured.

The Moore's house was in a well-established neighborhood with 1970s style homes. They pulled in front of what looked like a split entry model in red brick with white siding. The manicured lawn and tended flowers added to its hominess.

"This seems to be it," Christian announced.

"Ready?" Jewell asked.

Lydia nodded.

It was a warm, sunny day bursting with color. The sky was a bright blue, the grass and trees were lush with green and the flowers full of rainbow blooms.

Jewell opened Lydia's door, and they awaited Christian before following the sidewalk to the cement steps. The front door opened before they reached it.

A stout woman about five feet in height and round as a teapot stood with a welcoming smile. Jewell didn't think she looked much like a "Sadie." Plus, she predicted the woman had at least 20 years on Lydia.

"Sadie?" Lydia asked.

"Hey now, look how pretty y'all turned out. Get on in here. Me and Dad have been waiting for this day. Couldn't wait to meet Nate's family. Oh my, Lydia, I'd've picked you out a mile away. Nate looked just like you."

Lydia placed her hand over her heart.

They entered the foyer with hardwood floors and hardwood stairs — one set leading up and another down. She heard a television blaring at a deafening volume. They followed Sadie up the stairs, which landed them in the living room. Jewell scanned the place, noting the living area to her left with an opening to a dining room. Close to the entry of the dining room, sat an elderly man engrossed in the TV. She saw a kitchen to the right of the dining room. A wall blocked where the two rooms met. The house was immaculately clean and neat. A hallway was to her right, which she assumed led to the bedrooms.

"Come on y'all, make yourselves comfortable wherever you want." Sadie swept her arm across the living room. "Let me fetch you some tea. Do you want some snacks? Of course you do. Now, Dad cut that thing off. Company's here. I swear, sorry y'all."

Christian, Jewell and Lydia converged on the sofa. Sadie introduced the man as Ed, Breanna's dad. He turned off the TV with a groan and Sadie pulled a wooden rocking chair next to the sofa for herself.

"Now, how about those snacks?"

"No, thank you, ma'am," Christian answered. "We ate only a few hours ago and still have drinks in the car."

"Okay, but we're having hot chicken tonight for supper and I insist you eat with us. I won't see or hear of anything else. No one leaves here hungry."

"Oh how sweet," Lydia exclaimed.

But Jewell noticed a quiver of her mother's lip.

With no drink orders, Sadie settled into the rocker.

"I was surprised to get your call, but pleased," she began. "We hav—"

"I only just discovered Nathanael had been here," Lydia said. "That is, Jewell discovered it."

"That's right," Sadie said. "He told us his kin called him Nathanael. He couldn't tell us that before, but after everything changed, well then he could tell us everything. But, Nate was his name in witness protect—"

"Yes, you see, that's what I don't get." Jewell swung her arm and snapped. "I thought he must've been in witness protection. I figured he bore witness against the crime ring based on the way he was swept out of the correctional system and disappeared without a trace around August of last year."

"You're exactly right. He came round here sometime in August, but we didn't meet him until October. We knew nothing about him. He just seemed to appear from out of nowhere. When Breanna announced she planned to marry him, we were, well, honestly…alarmed. He supposedly was a financial advisor who worked from hom—"

"Ha!" Jewell said, then slapped her hand over her mouth, not meaning to interrupt or react out loud. "Sorry, it's just that he wasn't very skilled at managing finances. Please continue."

"You know, Dad, you can join in. Honestly." Sadie turned to her husband, then shook her head.

"What?" he bellowed.

"Cut your hearing aid up."

He lifted his hand to his ear and a high-pitched whistle rang until he made the proper adjustments.

"I'm telling them about when we first met Nate," she called to him.

"Yep, I liked him. You didn't."

"Now, it wasn't that I didn't like him," she directed her correction toward Lydia. "It was just that it was too soon, you understand. Swore they were in love and dying to get hitched. Now, I was skeptical about the timing, that's all. Didn't think she had enough time to get to know him proper. But in the long run, we grew to love him. Couldn't help it. Loved him before they married in December, before the truth came out."

"The truth?" Lydia asked.

24

"We learned he had been in the witness protection program after the fact. He admitted how saying he was a financial advisor was a front they gave him, you know, the program. So he was relieved when the officer assigned to him informed him they had busted up and arrested the leaders of that crime ring. That's when he decided to take his chances and leave protection. He stewed over the decision, and good, let me tell you, but the officer assured him Breanna and well, frankly, us too, should be safe. According to Nate, sorry, Nathanael, he never would've made enough money in witness protection to support a family and pay Jewell back."

"Pay me back?"

"Yep, he told us everything. He planned to pay you back the fifty thousand he owed you, and he planned to search for his mother. Sadly, he didn't get a chance to do either."

"Oh gosh," Lydia said. "Are you angry about his decision?" She held her breath.

"Nah, we knew his heart. He meant no harm. Wanted to make up for his mistakes. Can't fault anyone for that. The good Lord tells us to forgive. Don't get me wrong, we miss Breanna every day, but he was her choice."

"When he left the protection, that's when he secured the car salesman job?" Lydia asked.

"And obviously felt it was safe to be in the newspaper," Jewell added.

"Exactly."

"He was planning to pay me back," Jewell acknowledged.

"And he planned to search for me," Lydia said.

Jewell was certain they would all burst into tears until she heard a distant sound. She focused. It was crying. It was coming from the hallway and it was the cries of a baby.

Christian, Jewell and Lydia flipped looks back and forth.

"Is that?" Lydia asked.

"Oh dear, oh dear," Sadie said and glanced at Ed. "I'll be right back."

Silence filled the living room until Ed clicked the remote to blare his TV again.

Jewell nudged Lydia to look down the hallway as Sadie returned, carrying an adorable baby girl. She wore a yellow dress and a yellow headband that contrasted beautifully with her jet-black hair. She had the tiniest black tuft curled on her forehead. She grinned through the remnants of tears and kicked her legs in excitement.

"Oh my heart." Lydia grabbed Jewell's forearm. "Oh my heart. Is that…?"

Sadie made her way next to Lydia. "Yepper, this is your grandbaby. Now, give your other grandma some sugar, Olivia."

She handed the baby to Lydia. The little one fixed her eyes on Sadie and kept watch on her as she returned to the rocker. Once Sadie sat, the baby refocused on Lydia's necklace, reaching for it and pulling it towards her mouth.

Lydia giggled through her tears. She stroked Olivia's head. "Oh, you beautiful baby girl." She lifted her and pressed her against her chest.

Jewell and Christian exchanged glances and pouts.

"How old is she?" Lydia asked.

"Born June first. A little over three months old now. If you do the math…I might as well put it out there," she glanced back at Ed, who had clicked the TV off again, "that puts her conceived in September. What can you do?"

"Is her last name Miles or Caldwell?"

"Right, I see why you'd ask. Miles was the name for witness protection. Once out, he took Caldwell back. Though, I need to tell you the story. He moved Miles to his middle name. He—"

"He did?" Lydia snapped. She and Jewell flashed wide-eyed glances at each other.

"Yep, he told us the story of his grandfather. He got used to our

Sunday meetings with the Lord and learned a lot, even how to forgive."

They continued to visit for hours. Sadie had no trouble keeping the conversation alive. They watched as Olivia played on a blanket on the floor. Jewell held back as long as possible, then joined her on the blanket and shook rattles and sang. She lay close to Olivia and breathed in the sweet baby smell of soaps and lotions.

They learned more about Breanna and Nathanael until Sadie announced it was time to get her "hot chicken" and biscuits ready. "Dad's got a regimented stomach."

They had a pleasant dinner and discovered what the "hot" meant in hot chicken. Thank heavens for the biscuits. Lydia asked if it would be okay for her to feed Olivia.

"You kidding? We'll take all the help we can get. I was in my forties when I had Breanna and Dad in his fifties. We were older parents and now, well, we're ancient grandparents." She chuckled. "You're much younger, Lydia, plus you've got these youngins to help. Feel free to visit any time, and if you'd like to take Olivia on outings from time to time, you're most welcome. Honestly, we could use the rest, couldn't we, Dad?"

Ed looked up briefly from his plate and nodded.

Lydia turned to Christian and Jewell.

"Sure. We can come on weekends," Christian said. "And I'll feel fine bringing Johnathan now that it's turned out to be so relaxed and friendly here." He shot a glance at Sadie. "Oh, no offense."

"None took. We didn't know what to expect in Nate—er Nathanael's family either," she chuckled. "But, I gotta say, we're pleasantly surprised. Y'all are good people."

"You too," Christian said. "Now that we've been here, I feel good about Johnathan coming with us and that'll give Olivia a playmate."

"Perfect!" Lydia beamed.

They returned to the motel and Lydia announced she was exhausted and heading for bed.

"Want to go for a walk?" Christian asked Jewell.

"I don't know. I'm kind of emotionally exhausted myself, learning how Nathanael reformed and meeting my adorable niece. I think I fell in love with her."

"Me too," Christian said. "How about we go over to that gazebo and sit there for a bit?"

They sat snuggled and recounted the day's events until Jewell's eyes grew weary. Christian escorted her to her motel door and kissed her goodnight.

The next morning, Jewell heard a faint tapping on the door. She slid out of bed and slipped on her purple satin robe, thankful she had packed it.

She glanced back at the other double bed to see Lydia still sleeping.

A peek through the peephole revealed Christian dressed in camouflage shorts and a black T-shirt. She cracked the door enough to slide her lean body through and greeted him with a whisper.

"Mom's still sleeping."

"Ok, sorry."

They spoke in whispers.

"Want to go out for some breakfast and then a hike? I googled and there's a diner nearby." He glanced at her bare feet. "Do you have shoes? For hiking?"

"We'd better just go for breakfast. I don't want to leave Mom for long.

But, excellent idea, I'm starved. Let me change and leave her a note."
She closed the door to leave Christian standing on the motel patio.

When Jewell stepped outside and closed the door behind her, she caught a pink cast to her skin. She looked to the horizon. Bleeding pink and purple swirls on a light blue canvas painted the gaps between mountain peaks. She breathed in the stillness.

"I know, isn't it gorgeous? Another bright day ahead." Christian escorted Jewell to the passenger side of his car.

He drove to the diner in the middle of town. When they entered, Jewell felt an odd sense of familiarity. They stopped just inside after noting the sign reading: Please wait to be seated. As they stood pursuing the diner, Jewell felt a tug at her heart. She knew then. The place reminded her of the small-town diner where she and Nathanael used to meet for their birthday lunches. A tear filled her eye and trickled down her cheek.

"Oh no, what's wrong?" Christian asked.

"Not all my memories of Nathanael are bad ones."

Christian took his thumb and gently wiped the tear from her cheek.

The place was full of customers, and Jewell pegged most as locals. A good testament to the food, she figured.

"Two?" the broad hostess asked. "This way." She grabbed two menus, not waiting for an answer. They followed her to a wooden square table.

The hostess asked for their drink orders and pulled a pad from her apron. It dawned on Jewell that she must be the waitress too. Jewell, at first, took the woman to be in her fifties. Her hair styled in tight curls against her head, matted by a hairnet and with no makeup applied to her chubby cheeks. But as the woman, who identified herself as Sally, finally smiled, Jewell realized she was much younger than she had originally presented.

Christian ordered the number 2—two eggs, bacon, hash browns and buttered toast.

"You're getting bacon?" Jewell asked.

"Hey, when in Rome."

"Well alrighty then, me too. And some sausage."

"You rebel."

She batted her eyes briefly at him, then refocused her attention on Sally and the menu.

They finished ordering and Sally filled their cups from a carafe of coffee, then set it on the table.

"Well, not Rhita's, but drinkable." Jewell turned the sugar dispenser upside down and streamed the sweet granules into her cup.

"Now, how about that subject of our first real date?" Christian used air quotes for the word "real." "Say, wait a minute, this isn't it is it?"

"Oh, no," Jewell drew her words out for emphasis, "this definitely is not it." She raised her eyebrows at him. "But, hopefully, we'll get to it before we're married with kids." Her cheeks blazed as the words flew out of her mouth before she could stop them. Where had that come from?

"Hmm," Christian said, stroking his cheek.

"What're you doing? Come on, get a girl off the hook."

"I'm just daydreaming about little 'Jewells' running around the place. But you're right, we need a proper date. I accept the mission. It'll be my top priority as soon we're back in Florida."

Saved by the bell, Sally arrived with their order. She placed Christian's plate in front of him and then Jewell's in front of her, displaying eggs the way she liked them, cooked between over easy and over medium with just enough yoke to dip. Butter dripped from the homemade toast. Hmm, she calculated, one slice for dipping and one to slather with fresh strawberry jam, thick with chunks of sweet berries. She bit the one with jam first and the sweet/tart fruit tingled her tongue.

Christian spoke, drawing her focus back. "You know, I always wanted

30

a cabin in the mountains. For fishing."

"You fish?" She sipped her coffee to clear a bite of toast.

"Heck yeah, I fly fish and have been wanting to teach Johnathan."

"You fly fish?" She shook her head, conjuring a new image of Christian. An outdoors man?

"What's so hard to believe about me fly fishing?"

"I don't know. It's just not my first image of you."

"Well, it took me a bit to fall asleep last night. I seemed to have had someone on my mind." His eyes half-rolled as he nodded his head toward her with a grin. "Anyway, I figured since I've been dreaming of owning a cabin in the mountains and seeing how you have a niece here now, what better timing?"

Jewell stopped eating. "What! I'm speechless."

"Don't be. I'll call a realtor and we'll all come back up one weekend, including Johnathan, to look at cabins."

She felt tears well but fought them back. Only to have one escape when she smiled at Christian.

"It's just a cabin." Christian reached his hands across the table to find hers, then made her bust out a laugh as he made a poor attempt at a country accent. "Now, what d'ya say we gets us sum dis here strawberry jam to go and maybe even sum dat blueberry?" He scoured the room with a lopsided grin, as if searching the place for jars of the homemade treasures.

Jewell delivered a coffee from the diner to Lydia. "And look, jam." She held the two jars up and wiggled them.

Lydia drank the to-go coffee with one of her sweet rolls as she packed for their trip home. Despite their best efforts, they hadn't polished off all the pastries.

"How're you doing?" Jewell asked, filling her overnight bag.

"As well as can be expected, I guess. I lost my son, who I only knew as a small child." She inhaled a deep breath and slowly blew it out, her shoulders releasing with it. "But, I have a beautiful granddaughter. I have a new chance with her."

"Yes. Yes, you do, Mom." Jewell squeezed Lydia's shoulders from behind and laid her head on her back. Her hair was damp and fragrant with the scent of shampoo.

They loaded the car and headed back to Florida. The return trip started quietly until Lydia broke the silence. "You two make an amazing couple."

"Couple?" Jewell said with a wink, then flicked Christian's right shoulder. "We haven't even had our first date yet."

"Well, what are you waiting for?" Lydia asked.

"Yeah, what are we waiting for?" Jewell echoed.

"I know what," Lydia said. "I'd love to have an excuse to spend time with Johnathan. So why don't you two plan something for next weekend? I just happen to be free."

"Brilliant idea," Christian piped in. "I've had my eye on a particular event and it takes place next weekend and the following one. Now, no spying on the internet, Ms. Investigator," he warned Jewell. "I want it to be a surprise. However, I will tell you this much…you'll need a formal dress."

"A what?" She asked.

"Yes, a formal dress. You let me surprise you with the event and you can surprise me with your gown."

"I'm on it." Jewell pulled her phone from her bag and set out to compose a group text to the troupe. She alerted Lydia to follow along on her phone. Some time ago Jewell had added Lydia and Lynn to the group texts.

Jewell: *Shopping trip! I need a ball gown.*

Becca: *A what gown?*

Jewell: *For my first date with Christian.*

Della Rae: *I have the perfect place to shop.*

Gabby: *First date? Wait, aren't you on a weekend trip with him?*

Nicci: *She wants something young, Della Rae.*

Lynn: *Where are you going on this date?*

Candi: *I want to help.*

Jewell: *He's surprising me.*

Della Rae: *For your information, Nicci, my shop has young dresses!*

Sherry: *I bet I know where he's taking you.*

Della Rae: *Hush.*

Jewell: *Yeah, shhhh. It's a surprise.*

Z: *Wait, what'd I miss?*

Sherry: *We're having a shopping trip.*

Z: *Cool. When?*

Becca: *Yeah, when?*

Jewell: *The date is next Saturday.*

Becca: *Geez, plan much?*

Della Rae: *Okay, how about Wednesday before class? I'll arrange the appointment.*

Z: *Appointment? Fancy shmancy.*

Nicci: *I can't leave work early enough for shopping and then class.*

Della Rae: *Okay, then how about Tuesday and that way we have Wednesday if a second fitting is needed.*

Jewell: *Fitting? Is there going to be time?*

Della Rae: *Lort, I've purchased enough there, yes, they'll make it work. Besides, with your size, you may fit perfectly into one off the rack.*

Becca: *I can do Tuesday. Say 6 p.m.?*

Sherry: *Me too.*

Gabby: *I'm not about to be left out. Kevin can watch the boys 2 nights in a row.*

Della Rae: *Jewell? Does that work for you?*

Jewell turned from her texting and twisted her upper body toward the back seat. "Mom?"

"Yes, I can do either or both nights." Lydia had been reading along.

Jewell: *Okay, perfect. We're set.*

Maggie: *Hold your horses. I'm going on this outing. At least on Tuesday.*

Jewell's mouth fell open. She turned to Lydia. "Maggie almost never goes with us."

Finally, everyone texted their agreement confirming Tuesday evening at six p.m. with the backup plan of a second trip on Wednesday if warranted.

"Oh, I just can't wait," Lydia said. "And let's not forget shoes and a purse, and maybe a shawl."

"Are these subjects for my ears?" Christian asked.

Jewell and Lydia laughed.

"Nah, we can talk at home." Jewell stretched her hand to Lydia, and they shared knowing grins.

Three

Chapter 3

On Tuesday evening the troupe met outside the Pandora Plush Boutique and entered together.

A painfully thin woman, appearing to be in her fifties, greeted them. She wore a sleek black pencil dress with her hair twisted into a tight bun.

"Good evening, Mrs. Young," the woman said.

"Y'all, this is Bernadette and she is the best."

"Well, thank you," the woman said, barely parting her lips to speak.

Jewell gazed about in awe as the woman led them to the dressing suite. Sparkling crystal chandeliers lit the opulent room. A glass table showcased tiered crystal trays flaunting thumbprint cookies, china and stainless steel pots marked coffee and tea.

Z lifted a tattooed arm, inserted two fingers into her mouth, then blew out a long whistle.

"I've never seen a room like this before," Jewell said. "This dressing suite eclipses the shop we just passed through."

"Why, that's because they do the shopping for us, darlin.'" Della Rae fluffed her perfect jet black hair, teased as big as Florida and not a strand out of place. "All you need to do is relax and let them present you with selections."

"I've heard of places like this," Gabby said. "But figured they only existed in the movies."

Della Rae gave a swooping wave of her arm to coax the others toward the refreshment table. She led by example, selecting a small china plate and tucking a cloth napkin underneath it. She then placed three cookies on the plate.

Bernadette asked Jewell to wait in place for her as she prepared the dressing room to her right. She was left to watch her friends partake.

"Are you getting tea or coffee?" Nicci whispered.

"Neither," Della Rae whispered back. "They'll bring us champagne."

"Well, then." Nicci bobbled her head, springing her tight curls into action.

"La tee da." Even Gabby dressed for the occasion in something other than sweats or yoga pants.

The group followed suit, gathered cookies, then claimed cushy seats throughout the dressing area. Jewell shrugged. "Guess I have to wait here."

On cue, another woman wearing a plain black pantsuit carried in a tray of champagne.

Bernadette called Jewell into one of the walled-off dressing rooms, but not before she snatched a glass of champagne from the tray. Inside, Jewell noticed gowns of pink, blush, blue, yellow and burgundy hanging along the wall. The prim sales lady assisted her into the first over-the-top gown. She told Jewell she had selected these earlier that day based on Della Rae's descriptions of her.

Jewell stepped out of the dressing room and presented the first gown to the group. A light blue spaghetti strap gown with a slit at her left leg cut all the way up the thigh.

Her friends and mother cocked their heads this way and that to examine the dress.

Becca was the first to speak. "Nah. It's a pretty dress, but I don't think it's special enough. You'll be breathtaking in the right dress."

"I agree," Lynn said. "I think we'll know it when we see it."

Lydia nodded in agreement.

The next was a canary yellow dress. The bodice of the dress fit tight, but the bottom fell loose from her waist like a waterfall. It felt full and flowy and very feminine. The thick straps reminded her of a Marilyn Monroe dress. She stepped out to show her friends and mother.

"Why, I declare, I don't care if it is yellow," Della Rae said. "You're pretty as a peach in this one."

"It's better than the first one," Lydia said. "But I think we can do better."

Becca asked Jewell to turn around. She followed the command, adding a dramatic twirl.

"Let's see more options," Candi suggested.

Jewell retreated to the dressing room, feeling a little tortured and jealous of the others relaxing with their cookies and champagne.

A few moments later, as she pushed the dressing room door open, she heard Lynn gasp. She watched her nudge Lydia and nod towards the dressing room door where Jewell stood.

Lydia turned her attention to Jewell. "Oh, honey!"

Jewell eased past the dressing room threshold, still savoring the luxurious feel of the soft and pillowy material on her skin. The pink gown fell long and loose, caressing her thighs ever so slightly like the fingers of a gentle lover.

She stood just steps outside of the dressing room. The sudden and intense gazes gave rise to a flush.

Z blew out another whistle.

"Well, come on out," Maggie coaxed. "We can't see it from there."

Bernadette followed behind, lifting the back hem as Jewell cleared the rest of the doorway. Then, once positioned in front of her friends, Bernadette gently lowered the bottom of the dress and arranged it like a puddle around Jewell's feet.

She noticed Lydia on the edge of her seat, leaning forward. So she granted a warm smile and nodded.

Lydia leaped from her chair and rushed to Jewell's side. "It's so soft," she announced as she rolled the fabric through her fingers.

The others stood and crowded around Jewell.

"Oh, Jewell, I think this is the one," Lydia said. "Do you like it?"

"Yes. I like the subtleness of the pink."

Maggie stepped back. "From here, it's a pale pink with strong white hues."

"Yeah, that's it!" Candi said. "It looks white where the light hits most intensely."

"And I really love how the rhinestones around the middle showcase your teensy waist," Sherry said.

Jewell glanced in the mirror and skimmed her fingers along the rhinestones encircling her waist, then drifted to the choker-style neckline with matching rhinestones that pulled the halter top together. "I won't need a necklace with this."

"No, you won't." Lydia stepped behind Jewell, pulling her hair up to show off the neckline and halter-style top. "I'll style your hair into an updo."

"Please." Jewell turned her head this way and that to conjure the mental image.

Maggie circled Jewell, tugging on the dress here and there, then announced, "I don't think it needs a lick done to it."

"No," Bernadette said through tight lips. "It fits to perfection. That is as long as you wear shoes with three-inch heels, like the store ones you are wearing. May I wrap up the shoes as well?"

"No, thank you, I have the perfect shoes."

"My stars and garters, I think we have us a winner," Della Rae said.

Jewell changed back into her sundress as Bernadette prepared the pink gown for purchase. She happily joined her friends and accepted a second glass of champagne and a plate of cookies. "Don't mind if I do."

The night of the big date, Jewell stood, analyzing her image in the mirrors mounted on the closet doors. They allowed a full view of the gorgeous pink gown while Lydia buckled the strap of her silver shoe. Then Lydia stood and fussed with the twisted strands of hair falling from Jewell's updo, giving it an enchanting mystique. The rhinestone earrings and loose pieces of hair dangled harmoniously.

"They're here," Jewell announced, hearing a knock at the door. Her stomach tensed.

"Don't worry, he will melt at the first sight of you," Lydia reassured.

"Coming," Lydia called. "You wait here. You need to make an entrance."

She heard the door swing open and Lydia greet Christian and Johnathan. She took that as her cue to enter the living area.

She glimpsed Christian in a black tux. It was she who melted. Christian made a gesture as if he was falling back and clutched his chest. This caused Jewell to giggle, her nervousness vanished.

"Whoa," Johnathan said. "You look like the princess from my favorite movie."

Jewell squatted to his level and pulled him in for a tender hug. She then found it necessary to summon Christian's hand to stand back up in heels and a gown.

"You two go on. Johnathan and I have big plans. You're in our way."

"I have my cell if you need anything, Lydia," Christian said.

"We'll be fine. Get going." Lydia made a shooing motion.

When they reached the car, he opened her door and leaned in. "You are breathtaking."

Before turning the key in the ignition, Christian turned to face her. "I'm glad we're finally having our 'first date.'" He chuckled.

"Me too. Now, where are we going?"

"Patience, my dear. Promise me you didn't do any of your online snooping?"

"Scout's honor." She stuck two fingers in the air.

He drove toward the beach and she enjoyed the ride, still puzzled about where he was taking her. Then he turned into a parking lot.

"Hey, what's the big idea?" She teased. "This is a hotel."

"Ha. I said it was a surprise, didn't I?"

She pushed on his right arm, knowing he was teasing. She figured they would have dinner here and then he would take her to the actual surprise afterward.

He opened her car door, and she spotted other couples dressed in black tie and gowns passing through the main entrance.

"Hmm." She shot Christian a sideways glance.

"Patience. Didn't I request patience?"

"Well, I don't have any."

As they rounded a corner, the sound of music grew louder with each step.

The couple ahead of them opened the double doors and her heart skipped as her senses were overwhelmed by the buzz of the well dressed crowd and a big band blasting boisterous 1940s tunes from an elevated platform. The band was impressive, complete with trumpets, trombones, saxophones, and a rhythm section of guitar, piano, double bass, and drums.

She marveled over the beauty and elegance of the dynamic attendees.

The room whirled with electric energy.

They stopped at the entry table. Christian pulled two tickets from his breast pocket and flashed them to the woman behind the table who was wearing a low-cut black gown designed to spotlight cleavage. The woman acknowledged the tickets, then winked at Christian. Jewell drew back, crossed her arms and teased him with raised eyebrows.

"What? It's not my fault I look so good." He winked at Jewell. "Well, was this worth the anticipation?"

"Indeed," she responded as a host escorted them toward their table. A dance floor peppered with dancers of varying skill occupied the center of the room. The wall to the right encompassed the platform with the band. Tables arranged throughout the room sat draped in white linen topped with elaborate candle and flower arrangements.

They followed the host to an intimate table for two. Jewell gathered her gown and lifted the bottom as the host held a seat for her. Once seated, Christian leaned in and took her hands. He had to speak above the thundering music. "I hope it's okay. I had to place our menu selections when I purchased the tickets. Everyone has a set time and they prepare the dinner per the assigned arrival time."

She nodded, too busy taking in the scene to care about food.

"I know you're not opposed to red meat so we're having filet's, medium rare, sauteed mushrooms and onions on the side, asparagus with lemon butter sauce and salads with ranch dressing."

"Yum."

"Oh, and paired with a bottle of fine Merlot. Only, you must drink the bulk of it since I'm driving."

"Ummm, no problem there." She pointed her index finger at him with a playful wink and click of her tongue. She bounced in her seat to the music.

"Hey, wait a minute." She stopped and refocused her attention on Christian. "What about dessert?"

"I was wondering when you'd catch that. Cheesecake with fresh berries."

"Double yum! Hey, can we dance before it comes? They're playing swing. I can fake my way through that."

"We can." He stood and offered his hand. They quickly fell into their own version of swing with Jewell beaming at each twist and twirl.

"You're radiant," Christian said.

When the song ended, they faced the band and clapped along with the other dancers.

"It appears they're ready to serve our dinner." He gestured toward their table. "After you." Christian placed his hand on the small of Jewell's back along the rhinestone strip and guided her to the table.

"I'm having so much fun," she said.

"Me too."

"Do you think you could play trumpet with them?"

"I think they're a little out of my league."

"Hey, look. Those two are incredible dancers." Her eyes followed the tall, slender couple gracefully navigating the dance floor. It reminded her of the ice skaters she had watched as a child, mesmerized by the way they effortlessly glided across the ice. "They're dancing the quickstep."

"That looks ambitious. And tiring." Christian flashed her one of his flirtatious grins. "You know, this band comes around each year to this venue."

"They do?"

"Yes. What do you think about us taking a few ballroom dance lessons and we'll come back next year to give that couple a run for their money?"

"I love the idea. Only, I think it'll take more than a few lessons to give that couple a run for their money."

They enjoyed their dinner, topped off by dessert, then danced to the songs their skills allowed, mostly slow dances and swing.

Jewell's spirits dropped as the evening wound down, and the band announced their last number.

When they arrived at Christian's car, he stopped before opening her door. "We should probably kiss goodnight here. Lydia and Johnathan may still be up when we get to your house. I didn't mandate a bedtime for him, so if I know my son, they're still up."

"Well, actually…isn't your house vacant? Can't we go there?" She batted her eyes.

"No ma'am. You are correct. No one is there. But we aren't going there either."

"Why not? Don't you want to, um…"

Christian shook his head.

"You don't?" Jewell's heart sunk and her smile toppled to a frown. Was he not attracted to her? She thought he had been. Was he no longer? She fought a tear from forming.

"Aw, of course, I do. Of course, I want you. You're kind and intelligent and the most beautiful woman to grace that dance floor. But it's just too risky."

"Risky how?"

"Risky emotionally. Risky physically."

"I don't have anything," she answered, incredulously.

"I'm not saying you do, but suppose we make love. Then something, God forbid, happens and we break up. Then, there are other lovers and so on. It all adds up to too much heartbreak. Not to mention, too much exposure to who knows what."

"Is it because of your church?"

"In part, but it's everything all together. I don't want to hurt you or get hurt. It would already crush me if something separated us, but it would be tenfold if we were lovers. We can wait until we're married."

"Really? But what if we get married and we can't…it isn't fun? Or it doesn't mesh between us."

"Come here, you." He placed his hands behind her head and pulled her in for a fiery kiss.

She thought about resisting to prove a point. To spite him. But the warmth flooding her body and her complete abandon for how his hands wrecked her updo wouldn't allow her to resist.

When they stopped and her pink lipstick had smeared from her lips to his, he calmed his breathing and asked. "So, do you think there's even a remote chance it won't be fun? Won't mesh?"

She shook her head slowly. "No. I think it'll work. It'll work just fine." She paused. "But one thing first."

"What?"

"We need to wipe all my pink lipstick off your face unless you want Lydia to think you've taken a fancy to wearing women's makeup."

When they arrived at Jewell's, Lydia opened the door and informed them she had tucked Johnathan into her bed so he and Christian could sleep in her room and Lydia could sleep with Jewell.

Christian looked to Jewell.

"Okay. I'd love you two to be here in the morning." She used the back of her hand to shield a whisper to Christian. "Not exactly the arrangement I had in mind for tonight."

Christian made an announcement the next morning before digging into one of Lydia's elaborate breakfasts. "I've located a realtor in Tennessee who can show us some cabins. Can we go next weekend?"

44

"I can!" Johnathan said, which triggered the others to giggle.

"What? I can," he said.

"I know, buddy. I was counting on you going. I was wondering about Jewell and Lydia."

"And Romeo too," Johnathan said.

"Of course, and Romeo too." Christian chuckled.

Jewell seethed a bit. She hadn't slept much and thanks to Lydia's sleeping arrangement; she had to lay still. She had time to mull over the parking lot scene and it angered her more and more. Her pride smarted from Christian passing on her advances. She understood his logic of not wanting to jump into bed with her. Plus, the more she thought about it, it spoke volumes about his character. Nonetheless, it stung like rejection and she didn't appreciate him sitting across from her smiling and laughing.

"Fine by me," Lydia said. "Jewell? Are you okay? You don't look like yourself."

"I'm fine," she snapped, all the while glaring at Christian through narrowed eyes. She folded her arms. "I don't know if I can go or not. I'll have to get back to you."

She dwelled on earlier conversations when they shared their evenings, waiting for Lydia to leave her room. She recalled him telling her about some not so innocent escapades between him and Elizabeth when they were still in school. So that was it. He desired Elizabeth far more. He couldn't resist her before marriage, but he could resist Jewell. The blood rose in her cheeks.

"Jewell, what on earth would you have to do instead?" Lydia asked. "Come on. I'd get to see Olivia."

"Daddy said I can meet baby Olivia too, Ms. Lydia."

"I know, Johnathan," Lydia said, "and she'll love playing with you."

"But she can't play with trucks or things she can put in her mouth."

"That's right, honey," Lydia said. Then looked to Jewell and pleaded,

"Jewell?"

"Let her alone, Lydia," Christian said.

Later that day, Jewell heard her phone ping with a text. She swiped the screen. It was Christian, the picture of his bright smiling face in her contacts.

"Humph," she groaned before reading it.

How are you? Can we talk about what's going on with you?

Ha, what's going on with me, she mumbled to herself, contemplating her answer.

Nothing's going on, I'm fine.

No, you're not. My folks are here. Meet me at the downtown park.

Maybe I will or maybe I won't, she sang to herself but left for the park as he suggested.

"Hey," he greeted with his annoying grin.

"Hey, yourself," she said in her best sarcastic tone.

"Come on. Is this about last night? I was not rejecting you. I told you when we first got together, I can't do casual."

"You call what we've been doing casual?"

"No, not at all. But if we take it to a higher level and you leave. Then what?" He moved in closer, erasing the distance, and tried to take her arm. She jerked it away, wide for emphasis.

"What about you and your precious Elizabeth? You couldn't hold back from her. You couldn't save yourself for marriage with her."

For the first time, she saw him without his smile. She regretted her words. They stole his grin. Her gut hurt hoping she hadn't just blown this beyond repair. A million thoughts flashed through her mind within seconds. Was she trying to self-sabotage? Did she still think she didn't deserve happiness? Was it really so bad that he wanted to wait until marriage? After all, it was only her wounded pride talking. She marveled at his calmness.

"Did you ever think maybe Elizabeth is the reason I'm like this? When she abandoned us, it was painful, but if you leave—it would kill me. I'm afraid if I make love to you, I'd never survive losing you."

Jewell moved close and gently touched his arm. He took her into a tight hug.

"I'm so sorry, Christian. Let's never fight again. Let's go back to the way we were."

He didn't speak, but she could feel his muscles loosen.

The next weekend, they toured only three cabins before the choice proved clear. A cozy three-bed, two-bath model. It was a simple log cabin with a broad front porch and a door that opened into a living room with sturdy, plain furniture and an open kitchen beyond with a farm table to seat eight.

The past week brought another change. Jewell offered up her Beetle bug to Lydia and purchased an SUV to safely seat Johnathan and Olivia in the back. A vehicle with the highest-rated safety belts for Olivia's car seat and ample room in the cargo area for Romeo's carrier. She wondered whatever happened to the girl who drove with abandon from Washington to Florida in the sweltering sun with the convertible top down, all the while knowing this current life far surpassed that one.

The group spent many weekends in the cabin and it soon felt like home. Lydia had a room to herself, Johnathan and Christian shared a room and Jewell and Olivia were awarded the master bedroom with its own bath. The only time the sleeping arrangements changed was when Christian's parents, Caroline and Roger, accompanied them. During their visits, Christian and Johnathan made do in the living room.

One particular morning when they all were there, Lydia was up early again, cooking pancakes, bacon, biscuits and eggs.

Jewell carried Olivia to the kitchen. They were the last to arrive. Christian, Johnathan, Caroline and Roger had already taken their seats awaiting the delectable breakfast spread.

Jewell found it hard to believe how many months had passed since they first met Olivia, but now she was big enough to sit in a high chair. She joined the family, content to play with her toys while they ate. It didn't take long for her to learn the game of drop your toys to the floor and your grandmother will quickly and eagerly retrieve them.

Jewell shook her head. "Mom."

"What? She needs her toy."

"Uh-huh."

Jewell watched as Johnathan's little fingers worked to manipulate an egg sandwich he made by folding an egg up in a pancake. She resisted her instinct to reach over and assist him. Instead, she followed Christian's lead and let him work it out for himself.

She took her first bite, all the while keeping an adoring watch over Johnathan's efforts. He stopped and looked up at Jewell with pinched brows.

"What is it, baby?" She mumbled through a mouthful of food.

"Can I call you Mommy Jewell?"

Jewell froze. Her chewing came to a screeching halt. The others snapped their heads toward her.

Jewell felt tears welling. She swallowed the bite of food hard to clear her mouth and took a sip of coffee. When she laid her mug back on the table, she placed her palm against her chest and left her chair to kneel at Johnathan's side.

"Oh, baby, I would love you to call me Mommy Jewell," she looked to Christian who nodded in approval. She took him in her arms and squeezed him tighter and tighter until he said, "Ow, Mommy Jewell."

"Sorry."

"And, Ms. Lydia, I want to call you Bitsy."

They chuckled.

"Bitsy? But she's tall," Christian said.

"I know, but she's still bitsy like this." He brought his palms close together to show thin.

"Okay, we can't argue with you there," Jewell said.

Lydia beamed but looked to Johnathan's grandparents. "Is that okay with you?"

"Of course," Caroline said in a British accent stronger than Christian's. "I think it's grand." Roger nodded, too busy devouring Lydia's breakfast to speak.

With his grandparent's approval, she agreed to her new name. Lydia feigned a seated curtsy towards Johnathan, then turned to Olivia. "Did you hear that, Olivia? I'm your Bitsy."

Johnathan giggled. "Yeah." Then mastered his pancake egg creation and took a colossal bite.

Christian cleared his throat. "I have a request. That is if it's okay with Lydia or uh…Bitsy and Mum and Dad. I'd like to go on a hike with Jewell today. Just the two of us."

"Fine by me," Lydia said.

"Me too," Caroline agreed.

"Really?" Jewell asked.

"Yes. That is, if you'd like."

"I'd like."

It was a beautiful day. Jewell and Christian hiked for hours equipped with plenty of water, a compass, sunscreen and bug spray.

They were nearing a dead end Christian was told about. One with an incredible view. He had obtained the coordinates and used the compass to lead the way.

"Oooh, look," Jewell said. "I see it on the horizon."

"Indeed." Christian moved aside and swept his hand to gesture her ahead of him. "I want you to see it first."

She gladly obliged, then stopped when she got as close to the edge as comfort allowed. Her palms sweated from the height.

A peace came over her as she marveled at the rhythmic peaks and valleys of bright green. A lake lay at the bottom, still covered in smoke from the morning mist.

She whipped around to Christian. Only she didn't see him. A deep inhale filled her lungs with fresh air. Her gaze dropped, and she gasped. "Christian! What are you doing?"

On bent knee she found him, his arm outstretched. Sunbeams danced playfully off the glistening diamond.

They sped home to tell the family. Jewell's new ring fit perfectly on her left third finger. Christian admitted he had cunningly slid one of her rings from her room for sizing. It wasn't easy, he told her, what with her and Lydia always lurking about.

"So, Mom and your parents don't have a clue?"

They hurried down the rocky terrain.

"No. I wanted the moment to be between us. Plus, if you said no, I could save face, deny the entire thing."

"As if that was ever a possibility," she said.

The day finally arrived. Jewell was thankful for the forces of nature delivering the perfect setting. She drew in the beauty surrounding her. Shimmers from the radiant sun dazzled the sand, the sweet scent of roses and honeysuckle floated from her bouquet, and seagulls called above gentle guitar notes. The warm breeze brushed her shoulders, left bare by her halter-style gown.

She stood behind the makeshift curtain with her string of bridesmaids, made up of the troupe plus Maggie. They wore yellow. Her maid of honor, Becca, wore purple. Deciding to include the entire troupe posed a challenge for Christian who struggled to find enough male counterparts for his wedding party.

They contemplated holding the ceremony on Christian's sailboat, but the party and guest list had grown beyond the boat's capacity.

Tom appeared behind the curtain, covering his eyes. "Everyone decent?"

"We are," Candi replied. She then relinquished three-month-old Sophie to him. Candi's breastfeeding had nearly restored her figure to its previous shapeliness.

The day was unusually warm for December. Jewell was grateful given her gown was backless and her arms bare. The timing of the wedding was perfect since the adoption would be final in January. A new family about to merge: Olivia and Jewell Caldwell united with Christian and Johnathan Harrington.

Four

Chapter 4: Back to Current Time, September 2019

*O*nce the pitter-patter of tiny feet and enormous paws came to a stop, the house quieted. With the dramatic Halloween costume escape resolved, Johnathan, Olivia and Romeo lay on the floor in front of the TV. Jewell aimed and clicked the remote control to select one of the few programs that met her approval.

She slid closer to Lydia and placed her arm around her. "I know, Mom, Olivia is the very image of Nathanael. But that means she looks like you too."

Lydia blew out a reminiscent sounding breath. "I hope you're not too upset about Johnathan rejecting your bellydance costume."

"Nah. Besides, you remember how those costumed buccaneers at the Pirate Fest mesmerized him this summer."

"I remember that day well. In all of his excitement, he dropped the 'Jewell' part from 'Mommy Jewell' and you melted. He—"

The door knocker interrupted, sounding three sharp clacks. Lydia appeared as bewildered as Jewell.

"Hold that thought." Jewell crossed the living room to the foyer. She ascended the tiled platform to the double doors. When she peeked through the peephole, there stood a supermodel-looking woman, poised to drop the knocker again. Before the woman struck the clacker for a second round, Jewell opened the door to reveal all of the long, lean, nearly six-foot tall woman.

She wore a black button-up maxi dress with most of the buttons undone to reveal black thigh-high boots with laces as loose as the dress's buttons. She had swept her perfect chestnut hair into a loose bun, making a focal point of her obscenely full lips. Jewell shook her head, dumbfounded. "Yes? Can I help you?"

The woman's British accent rendered her self introduction a waste of breath. "I'm Elizabeth Harrington, Christian's wife."

"I'm Christian's wife," Jewell said, incredulously.

"Oh, of course. I meant ex-wife." The corners of her lips turned up slightly.

Johnathan approached and wrapped his arms around Jewell's thigh. "Who's that, Mommy?"

"Mommy?" The woman shook her head and slapped a hand to her chest. "I'm your mommy!"

Johnathan began to cry. Lydia quickly arrived at the door with Olivia in her arms. The woman's sharp eyes darted back and forth between Olivia and Jewell.

"Mom, can you take—"

Lydia nodded before Jewell had time to finish her request. With Olivia in her arms, she guided Johnathan away.

"You need to leave," Jewell said. "I don't know why you're here, but you need to leave."

"I'm here to see Johnathan."

"After all these years? I don't think so."

"It's not your decision. You have no rights."

Her words stung. Jewell slammed the door.

The woman spoke through the closed door. "That's fine, I'll just meet Christian at the University again."

Again? Jewell wondered. She watched through the peephole as the woman drove away.

Lydia returned with the two children at her side. "I heard the door slam. Are you okay?"

"Sorry, I shouldn't have slammed it."

"Yes, you should have," Lydia said.

Jewell knelt next to Johnathan and Olivia. "Everything's okay. There's nothing to worry about."

"What'd that woman want?" Johnathan asked.

"Nothing she's gonna get, baby. Nothing she's gonna get." Jewell turned her face up to Lydia. "Mom, is it okay if Christian and I eat dinner out tonight?"

"Sure it is. I'll make my homemade pizza."

"Yea, pizza!" Johnathan cheered, seeming to forget the rude visitor.

The next evening, Jewell arrived at Maggie's studio to find her wearing a white bellydance costume with a hip-hugging skirt.

"What's up with that?" Jewell asked Nicci.

"No clue," Nicci said. "Maybe it has something to do with learning a new prop tonight. You know how she likes to demonstrate."

Once all the students were present, Maggie began class with updates about her upcoming hafla featuring Aniela and Andrea, who were scheduled to arrive from California the following Friday.

Maggie had arranged for the troupe to perform in two numbers and informed them she incorporated the props they were most practiced at:

veils and canes. They were working on new props and choreography and getting the hang of them. However, Maggie said they weren't yet fluid enough to showcase in a performance.

Maggie conducted their warm-up, then instructed, "Okay, now fetch your Isis wings and sticks. But don't remove the wings from the package. Hopefully, y'all read your messages and were able to get two sets, one to keep here and a less expensive set for home practice."

Jewell marveled at how Maggie's southern accent amplified when she blurted commands. Their instructor's looks of sophistication, her long lean dancer legs and silver-gray hair didn't mesh in Jewell's mind with her accent.

"And remember, space yourselves with a wide berth, at least arm's length apart at all angles. I don't need any dang mishaps on my watch."

Jewell and Becca filled their spots next to each other, but before Becca spread out, she asked Jewell if she was feeling okay.

"Meh, so-so."

"Let's talk on the way to Rhita's," Becca suggested.

When the group was in formation, spread apart and holding their packaged wings, Maggie began with the background history of the style. "There's controversy and varying opinions on where the art of dancing with Isis wings originated. Some claim they came from showgirls and others claim the origin dates much further back. However, most agree the dance did not come from Egypt. Did y'all have time to watch the video I sent of Loie Fuller?"

Jewell said she had then listened as the others sounded their acknowledgments.

"I personally believe," Maggie continued, "that the concept of dancing with Isis Wings came from Loie Fuller in the late 1800s. She fashioned her silk costumes with pockets to slide rods into. This gave the illusion of wings. Then if you watch her dance, you'll notice her Serpentine dance looks very similar to the more modern Isis wing dance."

"I found her fascinating," Della Rae said. "I must've watched that dern thing a hundred times."

"Me too," Jewell said. "And I continued to read more articles about her. What I appreciate most was how she was not only a talented artist but also a scientist at heart. Did you see how she mixed chemicals to create color gels? And used salts to create luminescent lighting?"

"Yes, there's no question how truly talented she was," Maggie said. "Okay, although we've established the dance didn't come from Egypt, the name just might've. Look at the painted hieroglyphics on my floor and see if you can guess which is the goddess, Isis. Think about wings. Um...let's see"—Maggie tapped her lips—"the first one to find the painting of the goddess wins a coin scarf."

The troupe roamed the studio, studying the floor. With Jewell's photographic memory, she knew exactly where it was but wanted one of her troupe members to win.

"I bet this is her!" Gabby pointed at one of the painted images.

Jewell reached her before Maggie. "Yep, that's her. Excellent job, Gabby." They high-fived.

Maggie called the others over to the Isis painting. "See her golden wings? They believed her to be the moon goddess responsible for fertility, healing and above all, magic."

"Way cool," Z said.

"If you watched Loie Fuller's video and noticed her frenzied, wide sweeping arm movements, you'll understand why we focused on our shoulders and arms in the warmup. No one here has shoulder injuries, right?" Maggie used her index finger to scan the room. All shook their heads no.

"Okay, now, I'll demonstrate unpacking the wings. Then y'all will follow what I do. Candi, can I borrow yours?"

"See how they're wrapped in a tight spiral? You'll grab the outside end, hold them up above your head, like this, and release the rest of the material to fall gently."

A pastel rainbow of pink, yellow, and blue draped open in front of Maggie.

"Ooh," Candi said. "They're as pretty as the picture."

"Now, if y'all followed my instructions and ordered your wings per my specifications, you ordered traditional wings in the correct length to suit your height. You also should've ordered the rods." She scanned the group and nodded in approval. She showed how to insert the rods into Candi's wings, then handed them back to her.

Maggie grabbed her iridescent white wings, matching her costume. "Now, you'll pull apart the hook and loop strips of the neck-piece and wrap it around your neck with the closure in the front like so."

"They design your closure in the front for easy removal during your performance. We'll get into those particulars later." She waved her hands.

Maggie reached down, grasped the rods of her wings and extended her arms out to the sides, presenting a full wingspread.

"Whoa, that's so pretty," Candi said.

After a few struggles, the class wore their wings and mimicked Maggie's spread by stretching their arms out. Jewell felt pleased with the blue-green color she had matched to her peacock costume.

"Look, I can fly," Z said, spinning in circles.

Maggie clicked on theatrical sounding music and showcased the dance. She turned her back to the students and used the rods to flutter the wings into ripples as she raised them above her head. Then she turned back, wrapped like a cocoon, concealing her costume. She spun, gradually opening the wings to reveal the white glistening skirt and bedlah again. She dropped her right hand toward the floor and reached her left to the ceiling, executing a barrel turn. The spinning created a white iridescent wave.

Next she paddle turned in a circle, mimicking Loie Fuller's exuberant arm movements forward and backward so rapidly that all Jewell saw was the personification of a swan flapping its pure white wings. When her demonstration ended, the class cheered, and she took a bow.

"Okay, now, it's y'alls turn. First, roll your shoulders back and down. Lift your chest to the ceiling. We will sashay around the studio in an organized circle. Organized, Z. Did y'all catch that part? An organized circle. Those rods could poke an eye out."

The class chuckled.

"And I want you to play with the wings, lifting and dropping them, swirling them, whatever moves work. Improvisation is the creative way to dance with this prop."

The music continued as they circled the room. Jewell loved the feel of her airy new wings.

"Take your spots again," Maggie announced, "and I'll show you a few basic moves to practice at home. For now, it's mostly about getting familiar with your wings and how they move."

She performed as she explained. "You can use your wings to enter the stage dramatically. Take your right arm and bend it in front of you, just below your chin. Then take your left hand and swing it above and behind your head with your elbow bent. Now, all that's visible to the audience are the wings and your face. You're mysterious." She adopted a sinister tone. "Bahaha. No one knows what lies behind your cloak."

The class laughed.

"Perform a half spin to land your back to the audience, bring your arms out to the sides in full wingspread and spin. The audience catches hints of your costume until you stop in front, your arms reaching for the ceiling in full reveal with the glorious wings as a backdrop."

"And the paparazzi flashes blind our eyes," Z said.

"Ah…yeah." Maggie frowned. "Now, we'll make alternating figure eights with our arms in a fluttering motion."

"Y'all work on that. I'll come around to assist."

The troupe played with the wings, trying not to get tangled, all the while cackling and helping one another.

"Y'all, they're gonna hear us laughing and carrying on clear up to the street," Della Rae said.

As class neared the end, Maggie called above the noisy students. She clapped her hands to nab their full attention. "I want y'all to grab one of the hangers I set out and hang your wings neatly in the dressing room. Do the same with your practice set at home."

They moved to comply with her instructions when the studio door blew open, revealing a looming figure in the doorway. Dusk had set in enough for the streetlight to shine on her long, straight, bleached white hair. The bell sleeves of her dress hung down as she raised her arms, shielding her eyes as if being held in a trance.

"Seana?" Maggie asked.

"Yes, sorry for the interruption." She dropped her arms. "I need to speak with your girls."

"Concerning?"

"Can I join your group at Rhita's tonight?"

"All right," Maggie said. "Let me finish this, then once you've got your wings hung up, y'all just go on. But don't forget to practice. Oh, and Gabby, grab a coin scarf of your choice."

"Thanks," Seana said. "I'll go on ahead and secure a table."

On their stroll to Rhita's, Becca and Jewell lagged.

"You still seem a little down. I thought after we talked it through last night you understood Christian reaching out to Elizabeth. After all, he did it for you."

"I know, but I just can't get over him contacting her behind my back."

"But he explained he was afraid to tell you ahead of time. I can see why he'd be afraid to raise your hopes. What if she wouldn't consent? He knows how much you want to adopt Johnathan."

"I don't see why she even has a say. I showed Christian my research about abandonment and lost parental rights. But he said he's afraid of a legal battle and what that would do to our whole family. He already contacted his lawyer friend, Marcus Thornby. Do you know him?"

Becca shook her head. "Christian is right. You could go through with the adoption without her. But then what if she got wind of it and contested? What a hassle."

"I know. He's right. And I go back and forth between understanding and anger. What I don't like is him doing it behind my back. It just doesn't feel right. How do I know what else they talked about?"

"Because he told you what they talked about, silly."

"Yeah, I know what he told me but I wasn't there. And why did she come back to the States? Did their conversation over the phone go so well that she had to see him in person? Did they rush into each other's arms when she showed up at the University? Did they kiss? Who knows? Again, I wasn't there."

"You know Christian did no such thing." Becca giggled. "You have quite the imagination."

"Well, all this trouble she's causing and we still don't have her answer. Why can't she just sign the papers and go back where she belongs?"

"I know, I hate that part. But as far as Christian is concerned, he apologized, Jewell. He admitted he handled it wrong. Geesh, you two are the poster kids for happy marriage. Don't ruin my image. Heaven knows I'll never make it."

Jewell shot her eyes in her friend's direction and turned down the corner of her mouth. "You didn't see her. You'd know why I'm worried if you'd seen her."

"Hello. Do you have a mirror? You're beautiful and Christian loves you." Becca paused. "Hadn't you ever seen pics of her?"

"No, Christian never offered. It's not like he has them lying around the house. I guess I could've asked Caroline about her or asked to see her picture, but I really had no desire."

They entered Rhita's and found Seana at their usual round table.

Nicci scrunched her face. "She's in my spot."

They retrieved coffees and converged around Seana.

Nicci made a production of dragging a chair from another table.

"Are you quite through?" Della Rae asked.

"Has anyone been following the news about the governor's mansion?" Seana dove right in.

"I have," Gabby said.

"She reads gossip papers." Z rolled her eyes.

"No, I heard it too," Della Rae offered. "You know my Gil is a business owner downtown. So, he keeps up with what's going on. Well, that is, of course, when I don't have him otherwise engaged."

Della Rae lifted her napkin to fan herself. She had been dating an Italian restaurant owner who made a regular practice of whisking her off to his hometown of Amalfi at the drop of a hat.

"That's correct," Seana said. "Tourists are avoiding the mansion and spreading the word that it's haunted. I've become somewhat of an expert on the place since they've commissioned my services."

"It's apparently worse than the case in your studio," she continued, "This ghost is much more aggressive. There are reports of moans, banging pipes and even castanets sounding through the building."

"Castanets?" Candi asked. "Like our zils?"

"Similar, I believe. But the worst part..." Seana set her cup on the table and glanced side to side as she leaned in.

The group mimicked her and leaned towards the center.

"Yes?" Sherry asked. "The worst part?"

"Some visitors and...well, even some employees, say this feeling comes over them."

"A feeling?" Becca asked.

"Yes, a feeling." Seana continued. "A sense that someone is taking over their body."

"Ah!" Z exclaimed, pushing her coffee away. "Oh no. Count me out."

"What do you want us to do?" Gabby asked.

Jewell sat with the wheels of her brain turning. "We can start by capturing an image of the ghost and then research its identity. Like we did with Clara."

"Exactly!" Seana blasted, aiming her index finger at Jewell.

"I don't know, Jewell. It sounds a little scary," Candi said.

"Come on now," Becca said. "You know Clara won't let any harm come to any of us."

"Well, I guess we can start out and if it gets too spooky, back off," Della Rae said.

"Ha! I'll go," Nicci said. "There's nothing to be afraid of. How can you fear something that doesn't exist?"

"I can bring my camera," Sherry said. "When should we do it?"

"The sooner, the better," Jewell said. "Are there restrictions on when we can get in?"

"No, trust me," Seana said. "The Historical Society is ready to put this to bed. They'll welcome your help on any terms. They're talking about temporarily shutting down."

"How about tomorrow night?" Sherry asked.

"Saturday is better for me," Jewell said. "Christian will be there with the kids in case Lydia wants to come along. Besides, I guess I'd better talk this over with him first." Then whispered to Becca, "At least one of us talks things over."

"Me too," Candi said. "I need to discuss it with Tom. But as far as schedules are concerned, I'm happy to say any day is fine with me now that I'm a stay-at-home-mom." She beamed and sat taller in her chair.

"Tom's mother lives with us and is always eager to stay with Sophie."

"My, how the times have changed," Nicci said.

Despite the group's earlier reservations, Tom had turned out to be a suitable match for Candi. The others initially bet Tom's income as a mechanic would be a deterrent for anything long term between the pair. But since opening his own shop, he'd been able to provide well for his wife and daughter.

"Saturday works for me," Della Rae said. "That's Gil's busiest day at Bella Cibo, so I'm usually home."

"Can everyone do Saturday?" Nicci asked, taking count around the table. All spouted confirmation.

"Saturday it is then," Jewell said. "That is, with Tom and Christian's blessings. Morning is best for me. After breakfast."

The others agreed, and they set the time for 9:30 a.m.

"Okay, I'll arrange it," Seana said. "Trust me, the Historical Board will welcome any help. I've already bragged about how we joined forces and stopped the haunting at Maggie's studio. They're counting on our teamwork to restore the mansion to business as usual."

The next morning Jewell and Lydia cleared the breakfast table while Johnathan and Olivia played in the living area. It was open to the kitchen, so Jewell kept her voice low while filling Lydia in on the upcoming plans for Saturday at the governor's mansion.

She told Lydia that Christian hadn't protested the plans. "In fact, any time I tell him stories of Clara, he flashes me a patronizing grin. He's in the Nicci camp. Thinks it's a sham. When I asked why the staff at the mansion would go to such lengths for a hoax, he told me it was likely propaganda."

"What would motivate them to stage something to drive tourists away?"

"Not to drive them away, to drive them in. He said it was probably a publicity stunt gone wrong and now they need our gang to produce an even bigger show. They need us to put on a production of riding the spooky spirit so they can resume collecting admission fees and selling memorabilia."

"You can count me in," Lydia said. She folded the dish towel and draped it over the stove handle. "Okay, I've got to go out this morning."

"Meeting Sherry? She said you were swapping some morning meetings with evening ones."

"We are. Swapping some, that is. We're not meeting this morning. I just need to go out anyway."

"Oh. Okay," Jewell said.

Johnathan came into the kitchen as Jewell stood watching through the window. They watched as Lydia climbed into the Beetle bug.

"Where's Bitsy going, Mommy?"

"I don't know, honey. It's not polite to ask people where they're going," Jewell answered, all the while staring out the window as the Beetle pulled away.

"Okay." Johnathan seemed to accept her answer and returned to the living room.

"Yes?" Jewell said in a whisper to herself, scratching her head. "Where *is* Bitsy going?"

Saturday morning, Jewell and Lydia journeyed to the governor's mansion in the family SUV. They parked on the outer perimeter and trekked to the mansion a few blocks away. The excitement quickened their pace.

When they rounded the corner to the front of the mansion, Jewell spotted Maggie.

"Hey! You came too," Jewell greeted.

"I did. I figure I owe it to y'all for helping Clara move along. Although, I do miss the old broad at times." She released one of her belly laughs.

"Are we all here?" Becca asked as she and Lynn approached.

Maggie launched into a count. "Nicci isn't here yet."

"But I am." Sherry held up her camera case.

"And I'm here on time," Gabby announced.

"Okay. I say we go in." Della Rae motioned for others to follow.

Seana unlocked the door. It was closed to tourists for the morning. As they filtered past the threshold, Nicci caught up.

"I figured you decided to stay at home," Della Rae said.

"And miss this comedy show? No way."

"Where's most of the suspicious activity taking place?" Jewell asked.

Seana led them towards the basement stairs.

The group exchanged sideways glances and Jewell felt the hairs on her arms rise.

"Wait, can we start somewhere else first?" Maggie asked. "Ya know, get a little warmed up before going...down there?" She leaned forward and peered dramatically down the stairs.

"Sure, they've reported strange happenings throughout the place." Seana peered around as if sizing up the surroundings.

"Remember, it's best to take the shots into a mirror." Sherry removed her camera from the case.

"We wouldn't have found mirrors to aid us in the eighteenth century," Seana said. "They were made of speculum metal and ground to a shine. The mirrors found currently in the museum are our mirrors of today, made of polished glass. However, these are fabricated to appear like the ones from 1785."

"Fascinating." Jewell made a mental note to dig into more history about the period later on.

They began the tour on their current level, the ground floor. The Historical Society used grants, donations and government funds to fashion the mansion into a museum some time ago. They restored its rooms to resemble their appearance during the late eighteenth century known as the Second Spanish Period. The funds earned from tours went back into operations and the excesses went into the county pot.

Jewell had visited the museum on the weekend Kage insisted she do the touristy stuff around Southbridge with him. *Kage.* She hadn't thought about him for some time. But the memories from that fun day caused a twinge in her heart, if only for a second. After all, Christian was her lover, her friend, her rock. They were perfect. At least until the recent Elizabeth debacle.

The entourage, comprised of Seana, Maggie, the entire troupe, Lydia, Lynn and Miranda piled into the family's sitting room. Jewell recalled how the rooms on the main level were open for visitors, but how upstairs ropes blocked off access to most of the rooms.

"They used this space for the family to enjoy games and entertainment," Seana said. "The impressive fireplace straight ahead is constructed of coquina stone."

Jewell noticed the large mirror hanging above the stone fireplace.

Sherry gulped. "I guess I'll start here." She snapped in rapid-fire.

When she stopped, the group crowded around to view the images. Nothing but the mirror and bouncing light.

They inspected the remaining rooms on that level, the governor's office, the formal dining room, the casual dining area, separate sitting rooms for male and female guests and finally the enclosed porch. Sherry continued to snap photos throughout. After each room, the group examined the images and saw no signs of a ghost.

"Let's go upstairs next," Maggie suggested.

As they reached the top of the stairs, Jewell remembered that the ballroom lay behind the massive pocket doors directly ahead. Seana took one handle and Maggie the other as they slid open the doors to reveal the four-thousand square-foot ballroom. Jewell recalled the measurements from her previous guided tour. She imagined the grand parties the room must have supplied.

"Heavens to Betsy, would you get a gander at this," Della Rae said. "I guess I should've taken the time to check this place out before now."

"The ghost is bound to be in here," Gabby said. "This is where I'd hang out if I was a ghost."

"Only one way to find out." Sherry positioned her camera for action. "No mirrors though." She repeatedly clicked her shutter button throughout the room. They checked again. No useful images.

The ballroom was the only room not roped off on the second level. They marveled over the extravagant boudoirs. Sherry leaned over velvet ropes to capture images. Still no successful snapshots.

"Okay, I guess we have no choice but to creep down to the basement." Candi bit her nails.

"Well, I have a choice." Z turned to leave.

"No you don't." Miranda hooked her arm. "We're going too. Besides, there's safety in numbers."

"Oh, for heaven's sake. You babies stay here. I'll go," Nicci said.

"We're all going," Maggie said.

Jewell felt a chill and noted a musty smell as they descended the basement stairs. They were in no way grand or open like the staircase leading to the second floor. These were dark, dingy and narrow.

"This floor housed dorm-style rooms for the help," Seana explained. "The kitchen, the pantries, and the bedrooms are all simple and plain…utilitarian."

"It's definitely cooler down here. And damp too." Jewell folded her arms. She couldn't shake the unease coursing through her.

Jewell shivered as they approached a bedroom at the end of a hall. It was by far the largest of the rooms, a bit more decorative too. They found no mirrors in the other rooms, but a small one graced a dressing table in this particular room.

"I bet this one belonged to someone special," Jewell said. "Do you know who, Seana?"

"No, but I can find out."

"I'll do some online research too," Jewell offered.

Seana paused and stretched her arms out to her sides like brakes before they all entered the room. "I feel a presence here."

"Okay, that's enough for me," Z said.

"Me too, this time," Miranda agreed.

"Me three," Candi said. Several joined in as they headed for the stairs.

Only Maggie, Seana, Nicci, Lydia and Jewell remained. Sherry had handed Jewell her camera before darting off with the rest.

"I don't know about this, Jewell," Lydia said.

Regardless, Jewell stepped further into the room with trepidation. Her trembling hands pressed the shutter button. The others stood just inside the doorway. Lydia followed behind Jewell until they captured all angles of the room.

"All right, let's see what you've got," Maggie said.

Jewell advanced the images until they viewed each one. No suspicious exposures.

"I felt sure we'd discover something here," Seana said. "There's a strong presence."

Maggie's eyes widened. "Let's move on to the kitchen."

An entire wall housed the fireplace where a cooking kettle hung. A twelve-foot counter displayed food models of fruit, bread loaves and pies. Jewell snapped photos. "Maybe something will show up in this stainless steel workstation."

"Only one room left." Seana led them to the dining area where the house staff used to eat.

Task complete, they mounted the top of the stairs to find the others waiting. Jewell shook her head. "Sorry, no helpful images down there either."

"Unbelievable," Sherry said.

"It is," Della Rae said. "Mind if I look?"

Jewell handed her the camera.

"It's not unbelievable to me," Nicci said. "It was some fluke you all saw an image from the studio."

"We all saw?" Della Rae said. "You saw it too."

"Still, only a fluke," Nicci recanted.

They crowded around for a second run through of all the pictures. Nothing.

"What do we do now?" Becca asked.

"I'll start researching history," Jewell said. "It may give me some clues."

"Excellent idea," Maggie said. "Let me know if you need any help."

"Same here," Sherry offered.

They exited the mansion and Seana locked up. Jewell felt the warm sun on her face. The temperature had risen since they began their tour.

"I'm starving. Anyone else want to grab some lunch?" Maggie asked.

"Yeah, Rhita's," Z said.

"Or, I happen to know of a nice Italian place," Della Rae said and added a wink for clarity. "We can sit outside and enjoy the beautiful day this is shaping up to be."

Agreements ran throughout the group. "Bella Cibo it is," Della Rae cheered.

Jewell turned to Lydia, who hadn't responded. "Mom?"

"No, you all go ahead, I'll stroll around town instead."

"What? Why?" Jewell asked.

"I just feel like walking a bit. It's a pretty day. I'll use my app to summon a ride home."

"No way!" Jewell said. "I'll text when we're done eating and meet you wherever you are."

"Um…well…okay." Lydia bit her lip.

The group began their journey on foot to Bella Cibo.

"Geesh, what's up with Lydia?" Becca asked.

"It's her business," Lynn piped in.

Gil placed both hands over his heart when the dozen women converged on his place with Della Rae in the lead. He had the type of body that made customers trust his food. His sauce splattered apron clung tight to his rotund belly and his dark Italian curls lent him a boyish air. "Please," he said, stepping toward his private dining room.

"Wait, sugar puff," Della Rae said, launching her friends into hysteria.

"Yes, wait, 'sugar puff,'" Maggie teased.

"Alright, y'all knock it off." Della Rae continued, "Sweetie, we were thinking of sitting outside."

"Then outside it is," he beckoned his son. "Tony, please arrange the outdoor tables to seat these beautiful women."

Della Rae lingered behind with her beau as the others followed Tony.

"Hmm," Becca leaned into Jewell. "Tony is not too bad. Maybe *I'd* like a trip to Amalfi."

"Knock it off. What about Zachary?"

"Zacha-who-ry?"

Once arranged and seated, Gil approached their table with 2 bottles of Chianti and pitchers of ice water as Tony distributed glasses. "Allow me to bring a sampling of my tastiest dishes for you lovely ladies to share. I'll start you with warm bread and house salads."

They passed the family-style bowls of salad tossed in a homemade house dressing loaded with various types of olives and dried cranberries. When a breadbasket reached Jewell, she pulled back the cloth and fanned above it to soak up the delectable aroma.

"When are you going to start your research, Jewell?" Maggie asked.

"I bet she's itching to dive in," Della Rae said.

"You should be sitting beside her," Becca said. "She can't stop popping her knee up and down."

"Oops, I don't even notice when I do that. Yes, I am itching to dive in."

"Good luck there. I don't know what you think you'll figure out about some fake ghost from research."

"You'd be surprised what even the most subtle of hints can lead to," she answered.

"Duh, yeah. Remember when I was under suspicion for murder?" Sherry asked.

"The identity of the ghost" Seana replied, "will allow us to hold a targeted seance calling for the specific spirit who we suspect to be doing the haunting."

After devouring generous portions of Gil's decadent dishes, Jewell cried uncle. She placed her hand over her belly. "I can't fit another bite in."

"Me neither," Becca said.

"Della Rae, you are one lucky woman," Maggie said.

"Don't I know it. You don't have to tell me twice."

The group disbanded.

"Text Lydia," Becca said. "Mom and I will walk with you to catch up with her, won't we?" She turned to Lynn.

"Of course."

"Perfect," Jewell said. She heard her phone ping. "Okay," she answered. "Said she'd be on the corner of St. Anthony and King."

The three started on foot.

"Aw, remember when you lived on St. Anthony?" Becca asked.

"Yep, my cute little yellow house."

"Things certainly have changed since then," Lynn said. "But, for the better, I'd say."

"Far better." Jewell's full belly had put her in a better mood to count her blessings. "It'd be perfect without you-know-who."

"Yeah, Becca has been filling me in. What a horrible person."

"You know," Jewell said. "There's got to be something seriously wrong with that woman. Where are you in your studies of personality disorders, Becca? Because I researched them and studied the various aspects."

"Oh, I find them fascinating. Eek, sorry. I don't mean her. She's not interesting. Just the theory of the disorders. I know they can stir up gobs of trouble for those around them."

"You're telling me. So what type do you think she has?"

"Well." Becca tilted her head and looked to the sky. "I'd need more information to be sure."

"What if we get together with Caroline? She's known her as long as Christian. I bet ya she has more insight on Ms.Thing than him. You know how men are when it comes to beautiful women."

"I doubt Christian sees her that way," Lynn said. "After everything she's put him and Johnathan through. And now you."

"True, but let's get a woman's observations. Caroline is typically free during the day. What's your class schedule like tomorrow, Becca?"

"They're over at eleven. Then, I work in the bookstore in the afternoon."

"Perfect. Can you come by the house? Say around 11:30 a.m.? We'll have lunch. If it doesn't work for Caroline, I'll text you."

"You got it!"

Jewell spotted Lydia. "There she is."

"Do you want to come for lunch too, Lynn?"

"Thanks. But I have my regular hair appointment."

Lydia met them in the middle.

"Mom, can we throw together a lunch tomorrow for Caroline and

Becca if Caroline is free?"

"We can. I'll check the fridge when we get home. What's the occasion?"

"Information mining," Jewell said.

The four proceeded to their cars parked on the outer perimeter near the governor's mansion. Lydia and Lynn walked in the lead with Becca and Jewell behind. They reached Lynn's car first.

"Text me," Becca called to Jewell as they parted.

Lydia and Jewell continued toward the SUV. "Did you have fun?" Jewell asked. "You missed an amazing meal."

"It's okay. I just needed a little time to myself. Jewell, if I know you, you're ready to dig into the research."

"I am." Lydia's subtle subject change didn't go unnoticed.

"Well, I was thinking," Lydia continued. "Christian and I can take the kids to the park to give you some quiet time." Lydia halted her pace and placed her hand on Jewell's arm.

Jewell accepted the hint and stopped.

"Look, I know it's none of my business, but the tension between the two of you is noticeable even to the kids."

"I haven't said anything to them. I'm keeping their routine as normal as possible."

"Jewell, they're smart kids. Make your marriage a priority and work this out."

Jewell pulled in a deep breath and left Lydia to resume her journey to the car.

The next day for lunch, Lydia made a zucchini quiche and Jewell pulled together a Caprese salad with cherry tomatoes and mozzarella balls.

She drizzled it with a balsamic reduction.

"Hey," Jewell said as she and Lydia maneuvered about the kitchen. "We still have some of that ice cream from the downtown creamery in the freezer."

"Yea, ice cream," Johnathan called from the living room.

"Yea, cream," Olivia repeated.

"If you eat your lunch." Jewell peeked to see them sitting at the plastic table she had set up in the living room. They sat coloring now, but she planned for them to eat lunch there to give the adults privacy. She was careful not to discuss Elizabeth in front of them.

Lydia pulled a photo worthy quiche from the oven and set it on a cooling rack.Jewell leaned over to admire the thinly sliced zucchini sprinkled with cheese browned to the perfect gold. "That smells incredible, Mom."

"Thanks. Now, I say we cut some flowers from the garden for our tables."

"Me too," Johnathan said with his echo not far behind.

The three left for the backyard while Jewell set the table.

Caroline arrived, hugged Jewell, then turned her head this way and that around the house.

"They're outside cutting flowers for the tables."

"Brilliant. I'll join them."

Becca tapped on the door, then pushed it open. "Where is everyone? Whoa, look at that pie."

"It's a quiche. How were your class—"

"Aunt Becca," Johnathan ran to her.

With the kids eating and Caroline and Becca seated, Jewell and Lydia served lunch.

Jewell grabbed her notepad and pen and sat at the table, poised to write in between bites. She grew impatient with small talk and cut to the chase. "So, what was she like, Caroline? From the beginning."

Caroline patted the corners of her mouth. "Let's see. About two years after we had moved here, we got a call from some friends in London. Said they knew a family from Stratford who were relocating here and wondered if we would help acclimate them. They said they had a daughter Christian's age who would attend school with him."

"I'll never forget that first day we met her. We met the family at the country club for lunch. Clare and Gordan were friendly, but there was a tension about them. Elizabeth sat with her nose buried in a teen magazine. The kids didn't have cell phones or electronics to tune out their parents back in those days."

Jewell peered up from her notebook. "I know, I'm only four years younger than Christian. I buried my nose in plenty of books, back in the day."

Caroline continued. "She was a stunning girl for thirteen. Most had awkward looks at that age, but not her. She showed up looking like something out of a magazine herself. Too bad her personality didn't match. She ignored the conversation until Christian spoke. Then I watched her eyes move sideways toward him." Caroline blew out a lengthy breath. "This is the part I hate the most. I encouraged him to show her around. I told him to introduce her to the other boys and girls at school. It was the christian thing to do. He was Mr. Popular. He knew everyone, and they all loved him."

"I can picture that." Jewell thought back to her own junior high days and their stark contrast to Christian's. She struggled socially being from various foster homes with little guidance in these matters.

"Ice cream." Jewell heard a little voice from the living room.

"Yeah, cream." A second tiny sweet voice sounded.

"Hold that thought, Caroline." Jewell swiveled to stand.

"No, I'll get it, Jewell. You listen." Lydia left to scoop ice cream.

"This lemonade is superb." Caroline took a gulp. "Back to Elizabeth. It didn't take long for her to dig her claws into him. Slowly I watched as she pulled him away from his friends, from his outside interest until she had his world set up to revolve around her. The spring of his senior year, he bubbled with enthusiasm for the future and the comradery of his mates."

Caroline gazed ahead as if daydreaming. "Car horns beeped outside our door and he bolted enthusiastically each time. That is until she got wind of him running with his friends. I told her to let him have his fun. He was heading to university in the fall. She scoffed, telling me he was running around, drinking and hooking up with floozies. I laughed. Christian was responsible. I knew better. She didn't appreciate my lack of support for her theories and lectured me on how she was going to university just as he, and no one saw her running about irresponsibly. No, I told her that was the last thing anyone pictured her doing. Once they began their college studies, he was a goner. All he did was work hard in school and cater to her whims."

"Man, that's sad," Becca said.

"It is, dear." Caroline patted Becca's hand. "I think of the years he could have had without her. But now he has you, Jewell, and couldn't be happier. You know, I hate that she ever came into our lives and I feel responsible all the time, but at least she gave us Johnathan."

Lydia returned to the table with four bowls of chocolate chip ice cream.

"Ooh, the creamery?" Becca held her spoon up.

"Yepper," Lydia said as she settled back into her seat and scooped a bite.

"What was she like with Johnathan?" Jewell pushed her plate aside to move the ice cream front and center.

"Good grief!" Caroline peeked past the kitchen island to see the kids. "They're busy with their ice cream. She left it to the nursery staff to feed him in hospital and then as soon as they arrived home, she moved into the spare room leaving Johnathan with Christian at night and the nanny during the day. I was still working, but helped when I could."

"She didn't breastfeed?" Jewell asked.

"Are you kidding? She barely held him. That is, unless there was a photo op. At his baptism you wouldn't have known she was related until photo time. Then she'd say, 'Here I'll hold him,' smiled her fakest smile, then promptly handed him back."

Jewell feverishly scribbled notes. She slid the notebook to Becca. "Well, doc, what do you think?"

Becca drew her head back with a deep inhale, then blew out an exaggerated exhale, slumping her shoulders with it. "Whoa, I know we have a cluster B here." She shook her head. "I come up with a cross between histrionic and narcissistic." She took Jewell's pen and tapped it down each line of the notes. "We've got attention seeking, at least from one person we know of, obsession with physical appearance and how others see her, i.e. the photo ops. It seems she may perceive her relationships with others as closer than they really are. Like how she latched onto Christian, assuming he felt the same. That's on the histrionic side. Many with those personality types are annoying, but not harmful. Then there are the narcissistic tendencies I see. Now these are havoc wreaking to others. Seems she believes she's special and more important than—"

"Ha!" Jewell threw her head back. "As in, more important than me? You can say that again."

Caroline patted Jewell's hand and nodded.

"So the rest of the narcissistic stuff I see, or assume from various stories and behaviors..." Becca tapped the pad again. "Delusions of power and success, arrogance, expecting recognition from others as she exaggerates her abilities, complete inability to recognize others' needs or feelings—"

"That one there." Caroline tapped the notepad. "Yes, that is her for sure." She peeked at the kids again, now playing with their toys. "I can't see where she ever genuinely cared for Christian or Johnathan. Only what they could give her."

"Anything else, Becca?" Lydia asked. "Not that it's not bad enough already."

"Actually, there is more. They hold unreasonable expectations of others and feel entitled to privileges from them. Then there's this dichotomy of how they envy others, but at the same time believe others envy them. This jealousy can lead to massive destruction to assure no one has something they don't. As easily as they attach to an ally, they equally can attach to a perceived nemesis."

"I'm her nemesis."

Five

Chapter 5

*C*hanging her focus back onto the ghost hunt, Jewell exhausted every online resource pertaining to Southbridge's history. Nothing provided enough detail to identify a potential spirit plaguing the mansion.

The next morning she cleaned up the breakfast dishes with Lydia. "I ran out of online resources. I must buzz out to the public library. Mind if I go now?"

"Oh dear, can you wait for me to come back first?"

"Come back? From where? An AA meeting?"

"No, just running a few errands. Don't worry, I'll be back in plenty of time for you to visit the library."

"Errands again?" Jewell paused. "Okay."

Lydia returned to stay with Johnathan and Olivia while Jewell took off for downtown.

The familiar smell of books and clean air hit her as she entered the library. She wondered why she hadn't visited before. It had been years since she held a book in her hands. Technology had pulled her away from the visceral experience of holding the smooth cover in her hands and the pleasure of sliding her fingers along the edge of a page poised to flip to the next.

She spotted the history section and made her way to the local history. She was scanning the shelves when a man's voice startled her.

"Can I help you locate something?"

"Goodness." She placed her palm on her chest.

"Sorry. I'm Nicholas. The librarian. I didn't mean to alarm you."

"That's okay. I get deeply engrossed in projects. I just didn't see you. I'm looking for information on the governor's mansion."

"Here's a section featuring the first families of Southbridge over history and various books on the founding fathers and early settlements. Do you have a particular interest?"

"Well, it's a little embarrassing, but authorities asked my friends and I to assist in a…um…well a so-called haunting of the mansion."

"Yes, I've heard people visiting the mansion museum have been reporting strange happenings. In fact, I heard it's hurting business. You'd think it would help."

"How so?" She asked.

"People like a good Southbridge ghost story. We have shelves full of them."

"I'm sure. Still, the owner solicited the services of a medium and m—"

"Seana?"

"Yes, you know her?"

"She's well known around here. Probably the only real deal we have. That is, if you believe in that sort of thing."

Jewell leaned back to analyze his expression. "Well, what I was saying is...the Historical Board summoned Seana and my group of friends to help solve the mystery of the spirit haunting the place." She measured his response. He appeared interested, so she continued. "Then we plan to help the spirit move on. We've done it before."

He nodded. "If I may, I'd like to select a few books for you."

"Sure, that'd be great. I did a little online research before coming today. I couldn't find much. The only piece of interest I found was an article involving a controversy from long ago. It pertained to affiliates of a governor."

"Oh?"

"Yeah, in 1789, a woman vanished from the mansion. A Spanish General's wife.

Nicholas cocked his head, still eyeing Jewell. "Floriana Lucia Ramos y Montoya.

"Yes," Jewell's eyes widened. "That's the name. I read no one could prove it, but they suspected her husband of foul play. Maybe she's come back for justice?"

"You're in luck. We have a book with a collection of letters she wrote to her sister. Ones never sent." He positioned the back of his hand to the corner of his mouth. "In my opinion, she never meant to send them. See, the only mode of transportation to Spain back then was via ship and it was tricky getting mail delivered. Plus, considering the content of her letters, she likely didn't want them to fall into the wrong hands. Toward the end of her letter writing, she switches addressees. You'll see. Very interesting."

"Really!"

He squatted to reach a lower shelf. "I've read this several times. She came to Southbridge in 1788 a few years after the Second Spanish Period began." He pulled a hardback book from its spot and stood clutching it.

Jewell reached for the book, but he didn't relinquish it. He continued his monologue. "As I'm sure you discovered through your online search, they transferred Florida back to Spain through the Treaties of Versailles."

"Yeah, I know that from general studies in school." She held out her hand for the book to no avail.

"This book has compiled documents and photos throughout the Second Spanish Period." He tapped the book. "There are photocopies of her letters and drawings included in an entire chapter dedicated to her story. They preserved the originals at the University. I like how she doodled and drew on the pages. I find it fascinating."

"Me too." She turned up her palms, growing impatient.

Nicholas continued, seemingly inspired by Jewell's interest. "Reading her letters left me wanting for more information. The chapter featuring Lucia is by far the most interesting in the book. It inspired me to dig through additional history. I found that the wife of the Spanish Governor had summoned her here as an effort to preserve their Spanish culture and the Catholic religion."

"Where did they find her letters?"

"In an abandoned barn on a farm. They found them in a keepsake box in a tack cabinet stuffed behind leather bridles and breast collars. At the beginning of the chapter, Professor Cummings goes into detail about the technical aspect of the paper and ink, etcetera."

"Floriana, who you will see called herself Lucia, was from Andalusia. In the eighteenth century, they educated only women from elite families. However, Lucia's mother had been from a noble family, who saw to her education, including fluency in the English language. But when she fell in love with and married Lucia's father, Mariano Ramos de Cordoba, her family disowned her."

Jewell had to smile as she listened to Nicholas recant his studies. She knew another nerd when she met one.

"The Ramos y Montoya family danced Flamenco," he continued. "The story goes that a Spanish General caught sight of her dancing as a young woman and the image burned in his mind. But he left Spain to accompany the Governor to Southbridge as his first in command under the renewed Spanish reign. The First Lady announced she sought to boost the Spanish culture, for fear of losing it and Catholicism. Arguably to serve his own wishes, General Zia y Velarde, suggested she bring the then seventeen-year-old Floriana to La Florida to be his bride. If it hadn't been for the lofty status of Lucia's mother, she wouldn't have been eligible. Her parents had allowed her to refuse many proposals, making her a late bride at seventeen. However, I can only imagine they felt this marriage was too important to Spain to give in to any refusals.

Finally, he extended his arm and offered the book to Jewell, who eagerly accepted it. She ran her hand over the cover before opening it to delve into the pages.

"Why don't you sit." He glanced around. "Over there." He pointed to a table and chairs nearby. "You'll find her story starts in chapter thirteen. I'll pull a few other books for you. You have a form of ID, right?"

"What?" She looked up from the pages. "Oh." She nodded. "Yes, I have my ID."

"Great."

Without responding, she moved toward the chair, all the while flipping pages. Butterflies tickled her stomach as she read the introduction about letters written so long ago:

13
The Letters
PERSONAL LETTERS FROM FLORIANA LUCIA RAMOS Y MONTOYA (the wife of General Mateo Zia y Velarde)

The Southbridge Historical Society released the following letters to St. Francis University in 1968. Upon receipt, the library department converted the documents to microfiche. In September 2009, the library department digitally restored the documents included in this chapter and added them to this book's second edition. During the remastering process, they altered the writing slightly to enhance the readability for contemporary audiences. This process smoothed any imperfections such as stains and mold. They imposed the images onto a background similar to the original paper to square the edges.

Floriana Lucia Ramos y Montoya (1771-1789) lived in Southbridge, FL from 1788 to 1789. She was the daughter of Mariano (Ramos) de Cordoba and Margarita Santos y Montoya from Andalusia, Spain. These papers encompass letters addressed to her sister and later her lover. Of particular historical interest are the accounts of the masquerades and parades during Catholic feasts to promote the Spanish culture and religion.

During the Second Spanish Period, Spain's rule was losing its grip in North America to the British and American settlers, forcing them to grant land to non-Catholics. The population continued to grow in diversity, further diluting Spanish culture.

As with many historical papers, the path of these documents is not concise. The Southbridge Historical Society was founded in 1856 and soon after their formation, the Governor's bookkeeper turned over any unofficial documents of historical interest. Staff discovered the documents when the Florida Purchase Treaty ended the Spanish rule and the United States assumed leadership. They discovered the letters rolled and bound in the First Lady's sewing box. A torn note specified a landowner had found the documents while preparing his barn for demolition in 1791 and that he discovered these documents in a cabinet. The letters were reportedly within a wooden box behind various leather tack items.

Experts conclude the author wrote on laid paper made from linen rags using a quill pen with iron gall ink. Historians speculate the First Lady provided senora Velarde with the writing supplies, as these items would have been expensive.

La Florida
16 Nov. 1788

My dearest ~~sister~~,

My deepest ~~wish~~ is to write to you
~~to~~ share my life through letters since it
saddens me to say I may never see you
again. I must write in English as our
Mother taught us and told me to use
always in La Florida.

My heart broke when you watched
me board the ship. My smile – I faked.
I refused to have you see my great
sadness. I must tell you I lost my
imagination **and** dreams on that ship.
I can see no further past it. No future.
I know my duty to our country and so
I must do it.

Oh my dear confidant I spit at the
ground for the day he watched us dance.
I felt his eyes bore a hole through me.

La Florida, 16 Nov. 1788, My dearest sister, My deepest wish is to write to you to share my life through letters since it saddens me to say I may never see you again. I must write in English as our mother taught us and told me to use always in La Florida. My heart broke when you watched me board the ship. My smile~I faked. I refused to have you see my great sadness. I must tell you, I lost my imagination and dreams on that ship. I can see no further past it. No future. I know my duty to our country and so I must do it. Oh my dear confidant, I spit at the ground for the day he watched us dance. I felt his eyes bore a hole through me.

I implore you to find the Governor's letter and burn it. The First Lady had no right to listen to the General's request to summon me to this new land. He preyed on her desire to keep alive our Catholic faith and our traditions.

It is worse here and with him than I imagined. I struggle with how much to tell you but I cannot keep it to myself. The wedding was not so bad. It was performed at La Florida's beautiful Basilica in our traditional Wedding Mass. There was a celebration in the grand dining room of the mansion.

Later that night I trembled in my sleeping gown awaiting his arrival to my room. I was awarded the largest room on the lowest floor. The Governor's wife set me up with pretties not awarded the downstairs' staff. He entered the room with that same look from when he watched me dance in our homeland. Then he took me like a savage and it was horrible.

I implore you to find the Governor's letter and burn it. The First Lady had no right to listen to the General's request to summon me to this new land. He preyed on her desire to keep alive our Catholic faith and our traditions. It is worse here and with him than I imagined. I struggle with how much to tell you but I cannot keep it to myself. The wedding was not so bad. It was *performed at La Florida's beautiful Basilica in our traditional Wedding Mass. There was a celebration in the grand dining room of the mansion. Later that night I trembled in my sleeping gown awaiting his arrival to my room. I was awarded the largest room on the lowest floor. The First Lady set me up with pretties not awarded the downstairs staff. He entered the room with that same look from when he watched me dance in our homeland.*

Then he took me like a savage and it was horrible.

I do not want to scare you from marriage my younger sister but you must brace yourself. Think about the beautiful flowers from our farm. Think about the days we ran freely through the fields collecting our plants. That will get you through it. And remember it only needs performed rarely and once you receive God's blessing to be with child you will have your reprieve.

Pray for me to be with child this month.

Your beloved sister,
Lucia

I do not want to scare you from marriage my younger sister but you must
brace yourself. Think about the beautiful flowers from our farm. Think
about the days we ran freely through the fields collecting our plants. That
will get you through it. And remember it only needs performed rarely and
once you receive God's blessing to be with child you will have your reprieve.

Pray for me to be with child this month.
Your beloved sister, Lucia

The words and drawings transported Jewell into an eighteenth century Southbridge. She switched from reading Lucia's letters to reading a few of the other books Nicholas had abundantly piled onto the table. He included the history of Southbridge and its role in the development of the United States. Many included photos from the period and they filled her senses. She tried pacing herself to savor the stories in Lucia's letters, but couldn't help herself from digging right back in.

La Florida
25 Dec. 1788

Merry Christmas my dearest sister,

I must tell you of the most incredible occurrance last night. I can hardly believe it. My Lady requested I dance for the Christmas Eve festivities. Only I did not dance only to our palmas and cantor but also to guitar. The other news my sister is that I did not dance alone. A young soldier who recently sailed from Seville emerged as the dancer chosen by My Lady to accompany me.

The ballroom was dark. All that lay with light was the center of the dance floor. We entered on opposite sides of the room. I was directed to pause before entering the light and was told he was directed to do the same. A throaty warble bellowed. My head whipped towards the wooden instrument in confusion. Remember how we had heard tales of others dancing to guitar?

La Florida, 25 Dec. 1788 Merry Christmas my dearest sister, I must tell you of the most incredible occurrence last night. I can hardly believe it. My lady requested I dance for the Christmas Eve festivities. Only, I did not dance only to our palmas and cantor but also to guitar. The other news~my sister~is that I did not dance alone. A young soldier who recently sailed from Seville emerged as the dancer chosen by my lady to accompany me. The ballroom was dark. All that lay with light was the center of the dance floor. We entered on opposite sides of the room. I was directed to pause before entering the light and was told he was directed to do the same. A throaty warble bellowed. My head whipped towards the wooden instrument in confusion. Remember how we heard tales of others dancing to guitar?

A singer called out. Then like a peacock he slid into the light. My heart fluttered and the blood rushed from my head. Sister I tell you even at this great distance his beauty graced my eyes. He was so majestic and proud. The guitar thundered a sequence. He replied with the snap of his heels. The singing the palmas and the strumming heightened. He spun and danced to the center backward. He halted and dramatically turned toward me and posed again holding my gaze.

I took this as my cue. Hands above my head — I slapped my palms and I first tacón my heels then golpe into the light. When I was within a step of him I saw his head fly back as if struck by a punch. My lips betrayed me with a smile. Slowly we danced around each other. I felt a heat rise like never before. I heard the audience's praises. I must tell you sister I was hit with a sudden fear as I remembered my husband was in the same room. I shyly glanced away through the rest of the dance.

A singer called out. Then like a peacock he slid into the light. My heart fluttered and the blood rushed from my head. Sister, I tell you even at this great distance his beauty graced my eyes. He was so majestic and proud. The guitar thundered a sequence. He replied with the snap of his heels. The singing, the palmas, and the strumming heightened. He spun and danced to the center backward. *He halted and dramatically turned toward me and posed again holding my gaze. I took this as my cue. Hands above my head~I slapped my palms and I first tacón my heels, then golpe into the light. When I was within a step of him, I saw his head fly back as if struck by a punch. My lips betrayed me with a smile. Slowly we danced around each other. I felt a heat rise like never before. I heard the audience's praises. I must tell you sister, I was hit with sudden fear as I remembered my husband was in the same room. I shyly glanced away throughout the rest of the dance.*

When the music stopped and we stood close a wetness soaked my palms. He whispered for me to meet him in the back south hall when the sun shone its last light of the day. I struggled to hold my serious expression.

If you and I were together as I wish we were you would now ask me what I did next. I rushed to the south hall. I knew it was the worst mistake of my life. But my sister I felt more alive than ever before. He must have heard my clicking shoes because he emerged from the corner. We embraced.

He requested I give him the favour of one of my garters. He breathed the words. I reached up through my skirt trying to raise the hem very little. I untied one of my red silk garters and offered it.

When the music stopped and we stood close~a wetness soaked my palms. He whispered for me to meet him in the back south hall when the sun shone its last light of the day. I struggled to hold my serious expression. If you and I were together, as I wish we were, you would now ask me what I did next. I rushed to the south hall. I knew it was the worst mistake of my life. But my sister, I felt more alive than ever before. He must have heard my clicking shoes because he emerged from the corner. We embraced. He requested I give him the favour of one of my garters. He breathed the words. I reached up through my skirt trying to raise the hem very little. I untied one of my red silk garters and offered it.

He took it ~ brought it to his face and inhaled. He kissed it and slid it into his breast pocket. He repaid me with his fresh carnation. My breath caught. I slipped it into the top of my dress safely between my breasts. The petals brushed cool on my skin. Please tell me I am not wicked.

We heard faint footsteps and voices in the distance. I told him I must go.

He whispered my name while holding my wrists and pulling me close. I was surprised he knew my name. He said he asked another soldier for my name the moment the dance ended. Then he asked me to meet him at the Badilla abandoned barn the day after Christmas. I knew where the farm was. Sr. Badilla had built a new house and a second barn much closer. He told me to enter through the back of their property to find the structure standing alone and barren.

I asked when I should meet him as I withdrew.

He took it~brought it to his face and inhaled. He kissed it and slid it into his breast pocket. He repaid me with his fresh carnation. My breath caught. I slipped it into the top of my dress safely between my breasts. The petals brushed cool on my skin. Please tell me I am not wicked. We heard faint footsteps and voices in the distance. I told him I must go. He whispered my name while holding my wrists and pulling me close. I was surprised he knew my name. He said he asked another soldier for my name the moment the dance ended. Then he asked me to meet him at the Badilla abandoned barn the day after Christmas. I knew where the farm was. Sr. Badilla had built a new house and a second barn much closer. He told me to enter through the back of their property to find the structure standing alone and barren. I asked when I should meet him as I withdrew.

He called the answer as I ran away~ ~After midday dinner~ Something made me nod in agreement. He headed toward the corner from where he had emerged. It occurred to me I did not have his name. Valencio he called back before I rounded the corner.

Oh what a glorious name. Oh what a glorious man to be in love with.

I rushed back to the ballroom. My chest pounded. Was my husband missing me? I slid back into the room on the heels of a few servers. My eyes darted searching for him. He was nowhere to be found.

I wheeled around to the touch of a hand on my shoulder. It was My Lady with her ladies in waiting. My shoulders slumped and I clasped my chest. What a relief. She told me her intention was not to startle me. She told me the ladies were retiring to the sitting room and the men in the game room.

He called the answer as I ran away~After midday dinner~Something made me nod in agreement. He headed toward the corner from where he had emerged. It occurred to me I did not have his name~Valencio~he called back before I rounded the corner. Oh what a glorious name. Oh what a glorious man to be in love with. I rushed back to the ballroom. My chest pounded.

Was my husband missing me? I slid back into the room on the heels of a few servers. My eyes darted searching for him. He was nowhere to be found. I wheeled around to the touch of a hand on my shoulder. It was my lady with her ladies in waiting. My shoulders slumped and I clasped my chest. What a relief. She told me her intention was not to startle me. She told me the ladies were retiring to the sitting room and the men in the game room.

I tell you my sister I was never as relieved. I now lay in my bed writing to you anticipating sweet dreams of my dancer.

Good night and Merry Christmas to you.

Your beloved sister,

Lucia

I tell you my sister I was never as relieved. I now lay in my bed writing to you anticipating sweet dreams of my dancer. Good night and Merry Christmas to you, Your beloved sister, Lucia

La Florida
28 Dec. 1788

My dearest sister,

I trust you had a Merry Christmas.
The elaborate floral arrangements and
spicy incense of the Basilica delivered a
grand Mass. You know how My Lady longs to
keep our faith and culture alive. I fear
it is slipping. I have grown fond of her.
She did not know the damage her summoning
me would bring. She tries to make it up to me
through many favors and generosity.

I will tell you now what happened on
Saturday. Please do not judge me. I could
not bear to ever see disappointment in your
eyes. But I must tell you that I met
Valencio as he requested. I lifted my dress
as I trekked through a hacked path in
the briar. I arrived a bit early to find
him in the barn holding the scythe. His
shirt was off and his back glistened
from sweat.

---

*La Florida, 28 Dec. 1788, My dearest sister, I trust you had a Merry
Christmas. The elaborate floral arrangements and spicy incense of the
Basilica delivered a grand Mass. You know how my lady longs to keep our
faith and culture alive. I fear it is slipping. I have grown fond of her. She
did not know the damage her act of summoning me would bring. She tries to*

make it up to me through many favors and generosity. I will tell you now what happened on Saturday. Please do not judge me. I could not bear to ever see disappointment in your eyes. But I must tell you that I met Valencio as he requested. I lifted my dress as I trekked through a hacked path in the brier. I arrived a bit early to find him in the barn holding the scythe. His shirt was off and his back glistened from sweat.

I startled him. He was ~~surprised~~ surprised
I was early. He hurried to throw his shirt
on and I chuckled. I watched his body melt
with relief that I was not angered.

He told me he was surprised I came and
I asked him if he would think less of me
if I told him I never once considered
not coming. He took my hand and helped me
up a wooden ladder to what he called
the hayloft. I gravitated to an opening.
He said the opening is used to throw the
hay to the ground below. The view is
incredible over the lovely valley.
The December sun warmed me. He came
behind me and removed my lace shawl.
He kissed my bare shoulder.

*I startled him. He was surprised I was early. He hurried to throw his shirt
on and I chuckled. I watched his body melt with relief that I was not
angered. He told me he was surprised I came and I asked him if he would
think less of me if I told him I never once considered not coming. He took
my hand and helped me up a wooden ladder to what he called the hayloft. I*

gravitated to an opening. He said the opening is used to throw the hay to the ground below. The view is incredible over the lovely valley. The December sun warmed me. He came behind me and removed my lace shawl. He kissed my bare shoulder.

Jewell's phone sounded, and it jolted her from the page before she had time to finish the letter. It was a text from Christian.

Hey, when are you coming home? Dinner's ready. Should we wait for you?

Dinner in the middle of the day? She wondered. And what was Christian doing home so early? She checked the time on her phone. Without realizing it, she had immersed herself so deep into her books; she passed the entire day and now had to rush home for dinner with her family.

I'll be right there. 10 minutes...

She stayed to read the last paragraph of Lucia's letter.

I turned slowly and his lips met mine. He pulled my hair pin and I tossed my head. My hair fell loose and soft. I felt no shame. He guided me to the hay piles and I lay with him. Only it was not painful or dreadful in any way. I did not have to think of the flowers or plants. I gazed into his black eyes and quivered as we found each other's souls.

Your beloved sister,

Lucia

I turned slowly and his lips met mine. He pulled my hair pin and I tossed my head. My hair fell loose and soft. I felt no shame. He guided me to the hay piles and I lay with him. Only it was not painful or dreadful in any way. I did not have to think of the flowers or plants. I gazed into his black eyes and quivered as we found each other's souls. Your beloved sister, Lucia

Jewell rushed into the house, her arms loaded with books.

"What's those, Mommy?" Johnathan asked.

"The proper question is, what *are* those. These are books for Mommy to study." A couple toppled from her arms as she sprinted up the stairs.

"I've got them," Christian called, gathering the spilled books. She quickened her pace, noting Christian was taking two steps at a time to catch her.

Jewell tossed the books onto the bed. Christian tossed her onto the bed.

She stood and smoothed her shirt. "What are you doing?"

He sat up. "I'd like to make love to my wife again, someday."

"I thought we were running late for dinner?"

"We are, but suddenly, the sight of you erased any notions of hunger. At least for food, that is."

"I'm not in the mood."

"We have to fix this."

"I didn't break it." She stepped to the door, opened it and told him she was going downstairs for dinner.

"Sorry, guys." Jewell kissed Olivia's dark curls. Lydia had already secured her in the high chair with some tiny crackers to munch on. "You too, baby." She kissed Johnathan's cheek.

"J.J.!" Olivia called, kicking her legs. She had adapted the nickname for her older brother after hearing Christian refer to Johnathan by the initials of his first and middle name. They figured it was easier for her to master than Johnathan.

Christian came to the table, and they passed dishes of grilled chicken and vegetables. With loving eyes, Jewell gazed around the table at her family. She watched Christian during dinner and her heart softened.

She thought about the romance between Lucia and Valencio and felt a sudden desire for her husband. She realized that night they would make love.

Six

Chapter 6

The next morning after Christian left for work, and Jewell and Lydia tidied up the kitchen, the doorbell rang followed immediately by taps from the knocker.

"Goodness," Jewell said. "We're coming already."

She checked through the peephole. It was a delivery person with a plant wrapped in clear cello. She opened the door. "Hello."

"For Jewell Caldwell." The man tilted the plant to check the label.

"Harrington. But, yes, I'm Jewell."

She accepted the plant. "Do I need to sign?"

"No ma'am. Have a good day."

"You too." She closed the door with her foot.

"What is it, Jewell?" Lydia asked.

Johnathan looked up briefly from his play. "Pretty, Mommy."

"Oh, it has Travis' logo on it. How sweet. From Travis. I guess he still thinks of me as Jewell Caldwell."

She set the plant on the kitchen table and peeled back the cello wrap.

"It's pretty with its white flowers, Jewell."

"I know, I'm not sure what it is, I'll look it up." She buried her face in the plant to inhale the scent of the blooms. She lifted her shoulders. "Hmm, not very fragrant."

She paused and rolled her eyes from side to side to process.

"What is it, Jewell?"

"My eyes burn." Her chest heaved with deep pants.

"Jewell?" She watched Lydia's eyes widen. "Your face…"

"Ow! It burns." Jewell rushed to the sink and wildly splashed water on her face.

Romeo barked feverishly. She heard his paws stomp erratically around her.

"What's wrong, Mommy?"

She heard Johnathan at her side and felt him tug at her shorts. But her eyes burned too intensely to open them. She turned off the water. "Mom, call Christian. I'm getting into the shower. Tell him to come straight home. Call Caroline to get the kids. Johnathan, Mommy is just playing a funny game."

Jewell rushed up the stairs with Romeo close behind. She chucked a trail of clothes as she ran to the shower then climbed in before adjusting the water. The icy stream felt soothing on her face. When she exited the shower, she wrapped her hair in a towel, wetted a washcloth and held it over her eyes. She set it down only long enough to slip into her bathrobe.

Christian burst through the bedroom door, breathless. "Bloody hell, Jewell." He rushed to her side at the bed and guided her down, holding her shoulders. He eased the washcloth from her eyes. He gasped. "Sorry. I didn't mean to react. Does it hurt?"

"Yeah, my face and eyes burn."

"I called Nicci. Levon is on his way."

"How can he leave his patients?"

"Don't worry about it. He said he's bringing a shot."

"Probably a steroid. Did Caroline get the kids?"

"Yes, she's taking them for frozen yogurt and then the park. She said to text when you're better and offered to keep them overnight if needed."

"No. I don't want them away that long."

"We'll see. Did you know you had an allergy to certain plants?"

"I don't think it was an allergic reaction. Some poisonous plants can trigger these symptoms."

"I don't get it. Travis is your friend. Why would he send you a poisonous plant?"

"He didn't. I think we know who did. Wait a minute…" Jewell continued to hold the rag over her eyes. "She must have dug around and discovered my friendship with Travis. Maybe she heard about Sherry's case? She knew I would trust Travis."

"She?"

"Yeah, don't you get it? Your majesty from England is behind this."

"Elizabeth?"

"Who else?"

"Nah. She's shallow, but she's not a criminal."

"Ha! I don't think you know her as well as you think you do."

She heard a tap on the door. "Yes?"

Jewell dropped the washcloth to see Lydia ease the door open then instantly cover her mouth. "Oh, Jewell." She was next to her at the bed in seconds with tears in her eyes.

"Levon is downstairs."

"Send him up, Lydia," Christian said.

Moments later, Levon entered the bedroom. Nicci and Marc followed soon behind.

"Come over here," Levon directed toward the bedroom chair with a table next to it. He knelt and placed his thumb under her eye, tugging the tissue down. "Look left. Right. Up. Down. How's your vision?"

She squinted through the pain. "A little blurry."

He had her medical history since they had established him as their family physician. "Okay, everyone out." Then he looked to Jewell. "Unless you want Christian and or Lydia to stay."

"Yes, Christian and Mom."

"Okay," Nicci said. "We'll meet you downstairs."

"No, she'll be staying in bed," Levon directed. "Come back up in ten minutes and bring her a pitcher of water and a glass."

He administered the steroid injection into her left hip, then the tetanus into her upper arm. When Nicci returned with water, he gave her two Benadryl and a pain pill. "You can take one of each every six hours as needed." He set the bottles on her nightstand.

Marc returned with the detective, Mary Adams.

"Mary?" Jewell said.

"Took some finagling to get this top-notch one, but I got you your own private eye here."

Mary went to Jewell's side and flipped her spiral pad open. "What happened?"

Jewell described the events with Lydia's help.

"I know it's that bi—" she stopped herself. "*Agitator* from England."

Mary recorded information from Christian about Elizabeth.

"It may be difficult to trace, but I'm heading to Travis' now."

"I know she duped Travis. He would never hurt me."

"I'll see what he knows and be in touch. I hope you feel better soon."

"Okay, enough." Levon shooed the others out of the room. "She needs to rest and drink water. Jewell, keep the cold compresses on your eyes."

"I'll keep freshening them," Lydia said.

"Call me if you need anything else."

"Thank you," Jewell said. "Thank you, too, Nicci."

"I just hate this!" Nicci said. "Do you want me to go find her?"

112

Jewell laughed. The drugs were hitting her.

She dozed, but images of Elizabeth flashed in her mind and woke her frequently.

It took the next few days for Jewell to recover, but by Wednesday evening she felt well enough to attend bellydance class. She was running behind and ended up being the last to arrive. She had been receiving texts of encouragement from the group. It always amazed her how quickly word ran through the bunch. Still, she was happy when they all rushed to greet her.

Maggie placed the Isis wing instruction on hold to run through the hafla choreography.

"All right, y'all, our performance is this Saturday. Let's run through both numbers. Who forgot their veil and cane?" She held up spares of both as she scanned the room. "Very good. Y'all are reading my emails and remembering. Although, Gabby isn't here yet, so I'll just set these in the corner. Let's warm up."

The group settled into formation and warmed up following Maggie's lead. As if on cue, Gabby rushed into the studio during the middle of the warmup. Jewell felt pleased to discover her carrying her cane and veil.

They executed each dance several times until they all agreed they felt comfortable.

"Now, I realize this is the first time we've performed at the theater. Saturday night, direct your families to drop you off around the back. They'll enter through the front. If you're driving yourself, you'll find parking in the back. Now for the lineup. Don't fret trying to memorize it. I plan to email y'all a program once I complete it."

"I open with my fan veil solo. The Sacred Moon follows me, then Saphira's troupe, Lotus Dawning, next. Saphira follows them with her solo. Finally, fifth in the lineup is the Sisters of the Silk Veil—"

"And the crowd goes wild for the Sisters of the Silk Veil." Z cupped her hands to impart her cheering crowd imitation.

"As I was saying," Maggie placed her hands on her hips. "Y'all dance your veil number, then Aniela closes the first set with her thrilling sword number. There's an intermission where the guests can mingle and enjoy refreshments while the dancers make costume changes."

"After intermission, we start with the second dances of each troupe. First to perform their second number is Sacred Moon, then Lotus Dawning and finally, y'all dance your fabulous cane choreography. We close the show with Andrea's solo, followed by a duo featuring Andrea and Aniela. They promise us a fun surprise." Maggie winked.

"Did you catch that?" Nicci shimmied her shoulders. "We get to end the troupes' performances. I recognize we're not the stars, but we leave the lasting impression of the troupes."

"Yes, your cane number shines and y'all will wrap up the troupe performances on a high note. Now, what is the number one rule for heading out into the common areas between performances?"

"Cover up your costume—," "Cover up—," "Cover yourself up—," the simultaneous answers echoed through the studio.

"Alrighty. I see y'all do listen to me."

On the way to Rhita's, Becca asked Jewell how she and Christian were doing.

"Up and down. Up right now."

"Any word on her narcissistic majesty?"

"No, nothing. No more lovely plants. No requests to visit with Johnathan. The waiting's driving me crazy."

"Is she still here?"

"Yeah, according to Caroline, she is. She meets with her occasionally."

"Doesn't it bother you that your mother-in-law meets with her?"

"No, not in the least. She's trying to stay connected. She's our link to Elizabeth and her shenanigans."

"Oh, that is good then. Doesn't Elizabeth have to work? I thought she was some big executive driven by her career with no time for family."

"Apparently she can work from here. Caroline said she's renting a beach house."

"Great."

"Yeah, great." Jewell rolled her eyes. "The better to torment me from."

Once inside and situated with drinks, the group converged on one of the two round tables with enough seating for eight or more. Rhita's clientele had increased to the degree that the owners rearranged tables and added a second large round one.

Della Rae lifted her mug. "Skinny latte here. I'm down fourteen pounds."

"That's great, Della Rae." Sherry lifted her mug.

"Way cool," Z said.

"I agree. Cheers." Nicci lifted her mug and the rest of the group joined in.

Della Rae beamed. "How's your research going, Jewell?"

"I found fascinating history pertaining to a Flamenco dancer from Spain who lived in the governor's mansion during the eighteenth century. The poor girl disappeared from the mansion without a trace."

"Egad." Candi set her mug on the table and shivered.

"Yeah, that's kinda creepy. Do you think...as in..." Z made the slashing motion of a knife across her throat.

"Sure looks like it. It's odd for someone to have disappeared in that day and age, especially a woman."

"So do you think it's her?" Sherry twisted her mouth. "She's the ghost?"

"I think so. I just started reading letters addressed to her sister. I'll know more the further I dig in."

"I say you're on to something," Della Rae said. "Why, remember how unsettled our Clara was because of her murder? Now, keep us up to date, ya hear?"

"Oh yes, I'll be waiting on the edge of my seat." Nicci held up and twirled her swizzle stick.

"Who else is nervous"–Gabby swallowed hard–"about this performance?"

"Relax, we'll be fine," Della Rae said. "You know it's only ever our friends and families that show."

"Plus," Becca bounced in her seat, then sang, "Andrea is coming. Andrea is coming."

"And…Aniela, Becca!" Jewell said. "Aniela is coming too."

On the drive home, Jewell's phone rang. She answered through the bluetooth in her SUV. "Hello?"

"Jewell, this is Mary. I met with Travis."

"And?"

"He feels horrible. Says he plans to visit you. He remembers selling the plant. It's Euphorbia marginata." She pronounced it carefully.

"Yep, Snow-On-The-Mountain. I looked it up already."

"Says he warned her about the skin and eye irritation. She said she was planting it in a fenced area."

"Ha, 'she.' So you got her?"

"Not exactly. He says it was a short, overweight blonde with bobbed hair. Probably in her late forties. He didn't take her name. I cautioned him about selling without records. I'm sure I don't want to know his tax practices. Do you know anyone that fits her description?"

Jewell stared at the road ahead, thinking. "Nope. It doesn't ring a bell. I'll ask around." She paused. "I guess Elizabeth hired someone to purchase the plant, right?"

"Exactly what I was thinking. I'll let you know if I find anything else. Keep your eyes open for any suspicious activities. And Jewell, stay alert. I've directed extra patrol of your house." Mary lowered her voice. "Do you have any mace?"

"No."

"Stop by my house. I'll text you the address. I'll slip you some police grade. I'm concerned."

"Me too."

Friday afternoon, the kids played in the living room with their toys. Lydia spread her scrapbook supplies on the kitchen bar positioned to keep watch on the two little ones.

"Do you mind if I run upstairs and read more history regarding the mansion before Andrea and Aniela arrive? Their plane should land in a couple hours."

"I don't mind. We'll have snacks in a bit." Lydia lowered her voice. "Then I'll put you know who down for a nap and J.J. and I will carry on."

Jewell situated herself on the master bed. She opened her favorite book, the one containing Lucia's letters. The other reference books lay piled on the nightstand for easy access.

La Florida
16 Jan 1789

My dearest sister,

Latent blessing from the Blessed Mother Solemnity. I prayed for you and all my Cordoba familia to understand the depth and breadth of Christ's love.

My Lady gave us a glorious celebration for San Sebatian's Day. The streets were so full of cheer it brought her great joy and hope for preserving our Spanish traditions. I think they try to pattern the town after our Marbella.

My sister I tell you my eyes are more open now. I am settling into this foreign place and I see how different it is from our land. Many people make up this small community. There are people native to the area and there are African people with many skills who were freed from slavery. My Lady tells me of cash crops of indigo hemp and rum. She is proud of her husband and his works.

La Florida, 16 Jan. 1789, My dearest sister, Latent blessing from the Blessed Mother Solemnity. I prayed for you and all my Cordoba familia to understand the depth and breadth of Christ's love. My Lady gave us a glorious celebration for San Sebastian's Day. The streets were so full of cheer it brought her great joy and hope for preserving our Spanish traditions.

I think they try to pattern the town after our Marbella. My sister~I tell you my eyes are more open now. I am settling into this foreign place and I see how different it is from our land. Many people make up this small community. There are people native to the area and there are African people with many skills who were freed from slavery. My Lady tells me of cash crops of indigo, hemp and rum. She is proud of her husband and his works.

For the parade of our celebration I wore my dance clothes and a red carnation tucked into my black curls to remind Valencio of the night he gave me his. I draped my lace shawl over my shoulders against La Florida's winter chill. He wore his uniform and sped to my side in the procession. The crowd and exuberance hid our closeness. We meshed into the merriment of the others. I saw his smile and I knew it was for me alone.

We have met three times now. At the barn. I know we must stop. I implore you sister please tell me how. He is my heart. I wish you were here. No. I wish I were there and Valencio was ordered to serve in **Cordoba**.

Your beloved sister,
Lucia

For the parade of our celebration I wore my dance clothes and a red carnation tucked into my black curls to remind Valencio of the night he gave me his. I draped my lace shawl over my shoulders against La Florida's winter chill. He wore his uniform and sped to my side in the procession. The crowd and exuberance hid our closeness. We meshed into the merriment of the others. I saw his smile and I knew it was for me alone. We have met three times now. At the barn. I know we must stop. I implore you sister please tell me how. He is my heart. I wish you were here. No. I wish I were there and Valencio was ordered to serve in Cordoba. Your beloved sister, Lucia

La Florida
27 gan 1789

My dearest sister,

I am growing fond of the farm where I meet Valencio. I have started going out on my own throughout the week. It is different here. People think only of growing and keeping the land and of the commerce. They pay little attention to the whereabouts of the wife of a general.

I find God in the fields of this farm. It is here that I write to you now. I sit in the hayloft to look over the glorious land.

Some of the plants and herbs here are different from ours. Some grow in the winter. I am anxious to see the spring plants. I experiment with them and will report my results to you. I now have a friend. She speaks little english and no Espanol. We have named her people Cimarron which the British here call Seminole. My friend is called Chenoa - I write it as she sounds it.

La Florida, 21 Jan. 1789, My dearest sister, I am growing fond of the farm where I meet Valencio. I have started going out on my own throughout the week. It is different here. People think only of growing and keeping the land and of the commerce. They pay little attention to the whereabouts of the wife of a general. I find God in the fields of this farm. It is here that I write to you now. I sit in the hayloft to look over the glorious land. Some of the plants and herbs here are different from ours. Some grow in the winter. I am anxious to see the spring plants. I experiment with them and will report my results to you. I now have a friend. She speaks little English and no Español. We have named her people Cimarron, which the British here call Seminole. My friend is called Chenoa-I write it as she sounds it.

My friend is **blessed**. She is gone with child four months now. We communicate through gestures and she showed me a plant to help me receive **the** same blessing inside my womb. She led me to a field where my sister all I saw was fire. When I inspected the plant closely I saw how each stem held a cap made up of tiny pink blossoms. I hanged them to dry in the abandoned **barn**. I sneak jars of water to soak them in the sun so I can drink them and bring about a child.

My love Valencio and I have made a home of the barn. He brings wood and makes seats for us. He brings blankets for our bed and I hate when I must leave each day and return to the mansion. I shall write when I have more news.

Your beloved sister,

Lucia

My friend is blessed. She is gone with child four months now. We communicate through gestures and she showed me a plant to help me receive the same blessing inside my womb. She led me to a field where~my sister~all I saw was fire. When I inspected the plant closely I saw how each stem held a cap made up of tiny pink blossoms. I hanged them to dry in the abandoned barn. I sneak jars of water to soak them in the sun so I can drink them and bring about a child. My love Valencio and I have made a home of the barn. He brings wood and makes seats for us. He brings blankets for our bed and I hate when I must leave each day to return to the mansion. I shall write when I have more news. Your beloved sister, Lucia

La Florida
7 Feb. 1789

Oh My dearest sister

My Lady the Governor's wife made report of a great pain about her loyns. She told of a thrust within her womb. This is when I learned she was with child. About three months gone they said.

I have been hanging all types of plants to dry in the barn. I made her a tea. The midwife fussed and said I had no business in the room but My Lady begged me in. She accepted the tea and looked deep into my eyes as she sipped. She laid the cup back on the saucer and whispered thanks and blessings to me.

In three days she returned to the dining table still with child and her cheeks pink. We feasted. We ate bowls of garbanzo soup with chorizo y citrus salads y beef picadillo y cuba bread.

La Florida, 7 Feb. 1789, Oh my dearest sister, My lady the Governor's wife made report of a great pain about her lyons. She told of a thrust within her womb. This is when I learned she was with child. About three months gone they said. I have been hanging all types of plants to dry in the barn. I made her a tea. The midwife fussed and said I had no business in the room but my lady begged me in. She accepted the tea and looked deep into my eyes as she sipped. She laid the cup back on the saucer and whispered thanks and blessing to me. In three days she returned to the dining table still with child and her cheeks pink. We feasted. We ate bowls of garbanzo soup with chorizo y citrus salads y beef picadillo and cuba bread.

Later we danced in the ballroom. My husband does not dance. Valencio danced with me and I tried to hide my joy. I fear my husband sees my joy I have in Valencio. Pray for me my sister.

Your beloved sister,

Lucia

Later we danced in the ballroom. My husband does not dance. Valencio danced with me and I tried to hide my joy. I fear my husband sees my joy I have in Valencio. Pray for me my sister. Your beloved sister, Lucia

Christian entered the bedroom and broke her concentration. She slipped the marker into the book, then set it on her nightstand with the rest. She slid over onto her side, making room for Christian in the bed. He maneuvered next to her, and she wrapped her arms and legs around him.

"Aniela and Andrea are on their way. Her last text said they were at the airport in line for the rental car."

"Great. I can't wait to meet them."

The room fell silent for a few moments as they lay together. Until Christian spoke. "I received a call from Elizabeth."

"And?" Jewell asked, flippantly. She raised up on her forearm.

"She wanted to meet."

"Wanted to meet?"

"I told her I'd only meet with her if she included you. She said to never mind."

"Humph! Then what?"

"That was it. She hung up."

"Great, so we're no furth—"

Jewell's phone pinged. "Can you…" She playfully leaned her body over Christian's reaching for her phone on the nightstand. "It's Aniela. They're in our neighborhood. I thought they'd message from further away."

Jewell and Christian rushed downstairs. Jewell found Lydia working on her scrapbook project and Olivia up from her nap watching TV with Johnathan.

"They're almost here. Let's go wait for them."

They hurried to the garage, following Jewell's lead. Lydia carried Olivia. She pushed the button to open a bay in the garage. They crossed through it to the driveway, leaving the door open.

"I'm so excited," Jewell said.

"Me too," Lydia said.

"Me three." Johnathan giggled and clapped.

"How are your studies coming along, Jewell?" Lydia asked.

"Fascinating. But I haven't finished yet."

"Admit it"–Christian reached for Olivia–"you're dragging it out so it doesn't end. Like I do with my craft beers."

"Guilty as charged." Jewell raised her right hand and laughed.

An unknown vehicle rounded the corner and Jewell spotted Aniela's fire red hair from the passenger window. She bounced and waved until the car pulled in front of them and stopped. Aniela was the first to exit. Jewell and Lydia hugged their guests, then Jewell provided introductions.

"Whoa, you're pretty," Johnathan said to Aniela.

"I like him already."

Christian stood Olivia on the driveway and motioned for Jewell to take her hand. He helped retrieve the luggage from the trunk, and they all entered the kitchen through the garage. Christian pushed the button to close the door behind them.

"Are you sure staying in tonight works for both of you?" Jewell asked.

"It does." Aniela waggled her eyebrows and flashed a coy grin. "Gives us time to get caught up."

"Yeah, as in...what's this I understand about you meeting someone on your trip to Cairo?" Lydia said.

"Oh, that little thing." She gave a dismissive wave of her hand.

"Sounds like girl talk to me." Christian turned to Andrea. "How about a manly beer and manly talk on the deck?"

"Me too?" Johnathan asked.

"Okay, but light beer for you," Christian joked.

Everyone laughed except Jewell. "Not funny."

"Thank you, Christian," Andrea said. "I got more info on the new Egyptian boyfriend during our flight and drive than any man should have." He made a gesture imitating a gun to his head.

"Then beer, juice and the deck it is. Come on, men."

Olivia sat in her high chair with cut up fruit while the women gathered around the kitchen table. Aniela filled them in on her Egyptian romance with Khalid as Jewell and Lydia leaned in with keen attention.

When she concluded, Lydia gestured toward the sticky toddler then lifted Olivia from the highchair. "Someone needs her bath before dinner."

"Aw, how amazing is it you found Olivia? She is so adorable."

"She is." Jewell watched as Lydia carried her up the stairs. "I feel blessed every day."

"Does she ever see her Tennessee family?"

"There's only Sadie left. We're going on Thanksgiving. She loves to cook and with Ed gone, she welcomes the company. I think she stores up all her conversation and unleashes it on us." Jewell laughed. Then, she took advantage of being alone with Aniela to catch her up on the progression of her bellydancing and then on the issues with Elizabeth.

"Yikes, that's some psycho stuff."

"No kidding. Oh, and there's this other thing," Jewell continued.

"Other thing?" Aniela asked.

"Mom—"

"Not to interrupt, but I noticed how you're calling Lydia 'Mom' now. That's so sweet. You two have come a long way since California."

"Isn't that the truth? It's hard to imagine us any other way than we are now. Isn't that funny?"

"No. I think it's great. Now, you were about to say something. Sorry."

"Yes, so, she's been acting kinda strange. I know her routine like the back of my hand. Then out of the blue she changes things up."

"Maybe she tired of her routine?"

"No, it's not like her. Besides, she usually tells me everything and I have a strong inkling she's hiding something."

"What could she be hiding?"

"I don't know and I don't want to pry."

"Are you sure about that? It sounds like you want to pry."

"Gosh, you're right. It's none of my business unless she wants to tell me."

"Or, maybe there's nothing to tell." Aniela appeared thoughtful for a moment. "But…if there is something juicy…text me pronto."

They giggled just as the men reentered.

"Anyone else getting hungry?" Christian asked. "Where's Lydia and Olivia?"

"Getting sticky fingers and cheeks cleaned up." Jewell stood and retrieved a dishrag to wipe Olivia's highchair tray.

"Hey, where's Maya?" Aniela asked. "I kinda miss her hanging around my neighborhood."

"Hard to say," Jewell said. "She'll show up when she's hungry."

Later, they all converged around the kitchen counter as Christian seasoned the steaks and Jewell and Lydia prepared salads and beans.

"Wine for you lovely ladies?" Christian asked, pulling a bottle from the rack.

"None for me," Aniela answered. "I never drink the day of or the day before a performance. It messes with my spins."

"And wait til you see her spin," Jewell said. "None for me then either. I'll follow my role model." She winked.

"Are you two ready for your performances tomorrow night?" Christian asked Aniela and Andrea.

"These two?" Jewell said. "They're always ready. It's old hat to them."

"Still," Aniela said, "I get the jitters when they announce the number before mine and I realize I'm up next. I have to take deep breaths to center myself."

"You never told me that," Jewell said.

"We never got that far in our lessons."

"Your appendix and your friend's drama pulled you away," Andrea said.

"I can't say I regret any of it," Lydia said. "It brought us together." She smiled at Jewell, then turned to Andrea. "Help me set the table?"

The dining room was open to the kitchen, delineated by decorative pillars. Andrea and Lydia rounded the dining room table in the distance, arranging place settings and chatting in low voices.

"Do you hear that?" Jewell asked.

"Hear what?" Christian said.

"They're talking in French."

The three quieted and leaned to listen. Andrea and Lydia glanced to see them tilted toward the dining room and stopped talking.

"Nah, it's your imagination," Christian said. "Lydia doesn't speak French."

Seven

Chapter 7

T he next morning Jewell awoke with the excitement of her
friends being in town and the anticipation of showing them
around. In her elation, she almost forgot about Elizabeth.

She woke Christian. "Let's go downstairs and start breakfast before
anyone else gets up."

"You don't think we'll beat Lydia, do you?" Christian reached his
arms for a big stretch that ended with both arms around Jewell, pulling
her in.

"Knock it off. Let's go." Jewell stood and slipped her arms into her
robe, then slid her feet into her fuzzy white slippers. "Romeo will come
with me, won't you boy?"

"I'm coming too." Christian threw back the covers and dressed in
sweats.

They descended the steps to make out Lydia at the counter on her
cell phone.

"Gotta go. I'll see you tonight." She hung up.

Jewell's eyes darted toward Christian.

133

"I figured you'd beat us up." Christian said to Lydia and shook his head at Jewell.

She accepted his message to let Lydia's phone call go.

"Hey, Romeo," Lydia greeted. He ran to her, wiggling his entire body.

"Christian and I will make breakfast. You sit and relax," Jewell said.

"Deal." Lydia wandered to the kitchen table and gazed out the window while sipping her coffee.

After breakfast, Christian added the third-row seating to the SUV. They all piled in with plans to show Andrea the highlights of South-bridge. Aniela had visited many times as Maggie's guest, but told Jewell she looked forward to seeing the town through her enthusiastic eyes.

"First stop, my favorite downtown," Jewell said.

"Let's see if I can still remember your word for word description," Andrea teased. "The downtown with its Spanish influenced cobblestone streets"–he swept his arms out to the sides–"laid out like a…"

Jewell reached for receipts in her backpack, wadded them up and chucked them at Andrea in the back.

"…each square is…" Andrea paused. "Wait, each square is what?"

"I'm not telling you." She tossed another wad that bonked Andrea on the forehead.

"Good one, Mommy."

"Oops." Jewell realized her children were watching. She turned to the front and slid down in the seat.

They strolled around downtown. Jewell missed her daily walks through this ancient city and its unique shops and restaurants. When they came to the Basilica, Jewell announced she wanted to light two candles. She observed as Christian and Lydia shared confused expressions at her announcement.

"What? I've been reading Lucia's stories and they've prompted me to read about the Catholic roots here."

"Alrighty then, let's all go light candles," Christian said.

"You're supposed to light them for someone," she said. "With intention."

"Who do you intend to light them for?" Lydia asked.

"For Nathanael and Josh."

Lydia smiled and placed her hand over her heart.

They entered the church. Andrea dipped his fingers in the holy water and made the sign of the cross.

The group stood examining him.

"I'm Catholic." He shrugged. "No one ever asked."

When they left the church, Johnathan said his belly was making noises.

"You must be hungry," Christian said. "I know I am."

"Bella Cibo's?" Jewell asked.

"That might be a bit heavy," Lydia suggested. "I'll leave it to the three performers."

"You're right," Jewell said. "How about sandwiches? Ooh, I got it, my favorite shrimp po'boy at Oscars."

"Perfect," Christian said. "We can eat outside."

After lunch they drove to the beach, took their shoes off and walked in the sand. Jewell lagged with Aniela. "Are you okay? You got quiet."

"It's only...I witness you and Christian...and the two of you with the kids. And it, well, it makes me realize, I won't ever have that with Khalid."

Jewell put her arm around Aniela. "You can't be sure."

"Yes, I can. I'm not moving to Egypt and I can't picture him ever moving to the U.S. So, there you have it."

"I'm sorry." Jewell used the arm she had wrapped around her to give her a gentle shake.

"Don't be sorry. We're having fun and that's all it is. Besides, how many people can talk about their boyfriend in Cairo?"

"Not I." Jewell laughed.

The theater dressing room was jam packed and buzzing with music, female voices and last minute practicing. Bags and cases cluttered the floors and counters, spilling their contents of sparkling material, head dresses and makeup.

"It always makes me nervous when I spot some of the dancers practicing right before the show." Jewell squinted to focus on the blush she was applying to Becca's cheeks. "It gets me worried that I need to practice. What if I forget what to do?"

"You won't. We've got this."

"Is Zachary out there?"

"No, we broke up."

"What!"

"Yep. Know any cute guys?"

"Like you need any help." Jewell used her finger to wipe a smudge of blush. "Say, wait a minute…this breakup has nothing to do with a certain Parisian bellydancer being in town, does it?"

Becca gathered her lush chestnut hair into a fountain, puckered her lips and blinked rapidly. She garnered her best arrogant voice, "I have no idea to what you are referring."

They chucked. Jewell was grateful for the tension breaker.

Maggie appeared from among the chaos. Jewell's breath caught at the sight of her instructor's deep purple costume with the form-fitting skirt set low on her hips and crystal laden cutouts at the top of each thigh. Her long torso appeared to go on forever thanks to the minimalist bedlah pulling her breasts up high and center. Her generous stage makeup had her looking ten years younger.

A member from Lotus Dawning scooted past Maggie and approached Jewell holding a colorful square box. "Hey, Jewell, look what I have."

She lifted the lid before Jewell could stop her.

As if in slow motion, Jewell lifted her arm to shield her face and Becca maneuvered to stand in front of her. An explosion of multi-colored glitter dowsed the pair. Jewell clutched her chest.

Maggie rushed to them. "Are you all right?"

Jewell and Becca looked back and forth between each other and bobbed their heads up and down.

By then all the women in the dressing room had huddled around them.

Maggie turned and snapped, "Melissa, where did you get that?"

The poor girl stood stunned, still holding the box. "I...I. Some man handed it to me when I came back from the bathroom. Said it was something for Jewell to wear. Said she was expecting it. I...I'm so sorry."

Nicci approached her with a plastic bag. "Drop it in here. Jewell, I texted Christian to come to the dressing room door."

"Okay."

"Hang on," Della Rae said. "Let's get these clumps of glitter off you two. I mean, a girl likes to shine on stage, but you're gonna out do me in this shape. I always carry me some extra washcloths." She used a damp one to remove as much of the excess glitter as possible.

Jewell trembled as she handed Christian the plastic bag in the hallway.

"Oh, babe, I'm so sorry. Now don't let this ruin your performance."

"How can I not?"

"Look, I'm sorry I ever doubted you. I will confront Elizabeth and put her in her place. She needs to go back to where she came from."

"Hell?"

"You'd think. I plan to send her packing. Now, promise me you'll relax and enjoy tonight. Otherwise, she won."

She inhaled deeply. "Okay."

Saphira, the leader of Lotus Dawning, stood on a chair flinging her long blonde hair behind her shoulders. She placed her arms in front, palms down, slowly gliding them up and down. Her bracelets clanged as she shushed the multitude of dancers into silence. "Now, if you remain very quiet, I can prop the door open so you can hear the announcements and the music."

Her plan worked for about five minutes until various uprisings of commotion popped up. Some over last minute costume adjustments and others involving disputes over who goes left when the other goes right.

Saphira closed the door to block the noise from reaching the stage and the audience. When Maggie returned from her number, the pair huddled in the corner then announced their plan to take turns guiding the dancers to wait in the queue two numbers ahead.

Jewell felt an eternity had passed before Maggie came back to guide the Sisters of the Silk Veil to stand second in the queue. They had wrapped and tucked their veils tightly into the top of their skirts. For this number, the troupe would begin their dance wearing their veils, then during a spin, reach down to release the eye-catching silk in a dramatic sweep.

Saphira stood ahead of them, poised to follow her troupe.

As Jewell enjoyed Lotus Dawning performing a Cabaret dance, it sunk in that there was only one more number ahead of her troupe. The fluttering in her stomach made her grateful for Lydia's advice against a heavy lunch.

"Hey, where are Aniela and Andrea?" Nicci whispered.

"Lort, don't tell me they're a no show," Della Rae said.

"Shh. No, they're here," Jewell whispered. "They have a separate dressing area."

"La tee da." Candi assumed a haughty pose, hand on hip and head thrown back, streaming her long straight platinum hair behind.

"Hey, we better get into formation." Nicci arranged them in the order

Maggie had established for their first performance. She started in the back and arranged from back to front, shortest to tallest. Gabby, Z, Della Rae, Sherry, Jewell, Becca, Candi. Then Nicci, the tallest, hopped into the front spot.

Lotus Dawning exited stage right and Saphira entered stage left to a cheering crowd. Jewell's stomach knotted. She inhaled deeply and conjured a mental image of Christian and the kids in the audience. Then her throat tightened as she remembered Christian's parents were coming too.

With hands trembling, Jewell focused on relaxing her smile as Saphira bowed then jotted off stage right. Jewell reached in front to squeeze Becca's hand.

All was a blur until she released her veil to flow like the wings of a dove. Then she relaxed into the dance and enjoyed every remaining moment.

The second half of the show went off without a glitch. Saphira and Maggie allowed the massive group of dancers to crowd around backstage for Aniela and Andrea's finale. As Jewell stood in awe, she marveled at how they kept such a great secret from her.

There before her danced her friends, tossing flames from one to the other, spinning wildly until the flames melded into one fantastic blur. She heard gasps and oohs and ahhs from the audience and from backstage. Jewell realized then why Saphira and Maggie allowed the dancers to pile around to witness such a show. Their cheers did nothing to mask the audience's. She also realized why fire extinguishers lined the curtains.

After they exited the stage, the other dancers rushed to catch Aniela and Andrea before they reached their private dressing rooms.

"Hold up, y'all, we want to see you," Della Rae called to them.

The three troupes converged on Aniela and Andrea, congratulating them and examining their extinguished props.

"Can you teach me that?" Z asked.

"If you come to Southern California."

Jewell pulled her jeans on, stuffed her belongings back into the gym bag and located a hook to hang her costume. She'd retrieve her belongings before they left for the night. Her more pressing thoughts involved the buffet Maggie promised. With the performances behind her, her growling stomach begged attention.

"C'mon." She beckoned to her troupe. "Let's hit that buffet table."

"You're on." Z hopped sideways to the lead.

Maggie and Saphira had arranged for catered snacks from San Sebastian's. Jewell spotted the table full of goodies when she entered the lobby. They had set out the first round of snacks for the guests during intermission and now the second round for the dancers. Maggie knew some guests may nibble during the second round but had ordered plenty.

The three troupes surrounded the table and Jewell discovered the attendees gathered in pockets of groups scattered throughout the lobby. She spotted Christian talking with his folks. He held Olivia's hands as she repeatedly climbed his legs, then flipped over. Jewell couldn't hear her giggles, but clearly saw them. Johnathan was tapping his Granny's leg, presumably to take him somewhere. Christian finally noticed the dancers around the table and beamed at Jewell.

"Want some wine, chica?" Becca held up and wiggled a plastic wine glass.

"Why not? We're done for the night. Now, why do they make these plates so small?" Jewell flipped it back and forth to examine it, then strategically plopped a little of each food selection onto it. She managed to squeeze in empanadas of chicken, shrimp and cheese, fried cheese balls, sticks with grilled steak, corn cakes and rice pudding.

"Sssfit." Z whistled and Nicci used her elbow to signal a free high-top table. The Sisters of the Silk Veil stood gathered around the tall table. They laid their drinks on it and held their plates.

Miranda approached and bumped Z with her hip. "Impressive job." She high fived with Z.

"Marvelous job to all you beautiful dancers," she said. Jewell liked Miranda. There was a serene sweetness about her.

Jewell bit into a hot cheese ball, causing it to ooze down the side of her mouth. She dabbed the corner of her mouth as she scanned the room. "Where's Lydia?"

More performers meant more attendees. With the crowd, Jewell had to maneuver to see around the various clusters.

Through a mouth full of food, Sherry said, "There they are." Then her eyes widened.

"They?" Jewell questioned Sherry's choice of word until she spotted Lydia paired off with a man. "Who's that?"

The rest of the troupe snapped their heads in Lydia and the man's direction.

Gabby squinted. "Oh, he's my insurance man."

"Your insurance man?" Jewell asked. "Who's he here for?"

Gabby peered throughout the room. "His daughter is around my age, but she wasn't in the performance. I don't see her anywhere. Beats me who he's here for."

"Hey, why is mom straightening his collar?"

"Ooh la la, I'd say we've got us a romance." Then Z sang, "Lydia and insurance man sitting in a tre—"

"Knock it off," Jewell teased. "Miranda what do you know about this? Were they sitting together during the performance?"

Miranda threw her hands in the air. "I have no idea."

141

Jewell waved erratically, trying to grab Christian's attention. It didn't work.

"So what if she has a boyfriend?" Becca asked. Jewell eyed sauce from the steak on her cheek.

"You've got…" Jewell took her napkin and wiped Becca's cheek. "There goes your blush."

"George!" Gabby blurted as she picked up her wine for a sip. "His name is George something. Kevin will know. Only he's retired now."

"You don't say." Jewell scrunched her lips. "A retired insurance man."

Aniela approached the table. "The performance is over, it's wine o'clock." She wiggled her glass.

"Whatcha make of that." Jewell nodded toward Lydia and the man.

"Whoa." Aniela pursed her lips. "I think we may have solved your mystery. Changing her routine, acting secretive, running errands…"

Sherry kept her head down, focused on her plate and her sweet tea. Jewell eyed her suspiciously. "Sherry." She drew out her name.

"What?" Sherry asked hesitantly.

"What do you know about this?"

"It's not for me to say. It's for Lydia to tell you what and how much she wants."

Jewell's eyes dropped to the floor.

"Look, she's obligated to discuss things with me. I'm her sponsor. She wanted to have something of her own, plus she was a little afraid of how you'd react."

"How I'd react? I don't react."

Z spit her drink. The troupe snapped glances from one to the other.

"Are you saying I react?"

"Overreact!" Becca coughed the words.

"Ha!"

"That's all right, darlin.'" Della Rae smiled her warmest smile. "It just means you're a true Southern belle."

The group laughed; Jewell included.

"I guess she is a big girl. I just thought we told each other everything. C'mon, let's go see our families."

They branched out. As Jewell reached Christian, the kids and his parents, she caught Lydia glancing over at her, cautiously.

Caroline applauded Jewell and Roger nodded.

"Mommy, you were the best of all."

"You really were." Christian kissed her.

"You all are biased."

Caroline took Jewell's arm and whispered, "I'm so sorry about the box."

Jewell flicked her eyes to the ceiling.

"So, what do you know about them, Christian?" She flashed her eyes toward Lydia.

"First I learned of it." He puffed out his cheeks.

"Yeah, he's Bitsy's friend. Mr. George."

"Is he really?"

Lydia and the man walked toward them. Jewell studied him as they approached. He was handsome with graying temples and a neatly groomed gray goatee. He appeared fit. Probably in his sixties.

"Hi," Lydia greeted. "You were magnificent on stage. Despite everything."

"You really were," the man said.

Jewell's eyes darted in his direction.

Lydia ran her hand down Jewell's arm. "Jewell, this is George Greenwood."

"Nice to meet you." Jewell extended her hand and drowned out the plethora of sarcastic remarks bombarding her mind.

Lydia, Christian, Caroline and Roger relaxed collectively when nothing else shot out of Jewell's mouth.

"I guess we'll call it a night," George said.

143

"I'm riding home with George. You all go on without me." Lydia kissed Johnathan and Olivia.

"I'll walk with mommy to the dressing room, you and Olivia go with Granny and Paps." Christian gripped Jewell's upper arm to guide her to the dressing room.

"Ouch. I'm not going to say anything sarcastic to them."

"Really?" He cocked his head back to view her.

"Really. I think it's great. I just wish she hadn't kept it a secret."

"Maybe she was afraid of how you'd react."

"Why does everyone keep saying that?"

Eight

Chapter 8

niela and Andrea returned to California. Their departure compounded Jewell's post-performance let down and left her with way too much time on her hands. Inevitably, thoughts of Elizabeth and her menacing flooded back in. Mary had picked up the glitter box from Christian and interviewed Melissa and other troupe members.

A bright sunny morning found Lydia and the kids playing in the backyard, tossing a ball to Romeo. Olivia giggled and ran in the opposite direction every time they tossed the ball. This launched Lydia into gleeful outbursts. The contrast of their joy and Jewell's gloom compelled her to withdraw.

"Mind if I go upstairs and read?"

"No." Lydia held her palm out, coaxing Romeo to drop the ball. "Go ahead. We're good."

Jewell settled in upstairs and immersed herself into more reading. She stretched the books out over the bed, resolved to wrap up this project and prove Lucia was the ghost haunting the mansion.

La Florida
26 Feb. 1789

My dearest sister,

I have clearly won the affection of
My Lady. She knows of how I helped her.
The life inside of her grows steadily and she
barely hides it under her silk mantua.

Please feel comfort in how I am adjusting
to this new home. Without My Lady and
Valencio and Chenoa my heart would be lost.
I still miss you and our Madre and Padre and
our seven little sisters. Only it is a little
better now.

Spring has arrived. The herbs flourish.
I discover a new one each day and **Chenoa**
helps me understand them. I fear my abandoned
fields will be taken over by men to grow
indigo. There is great demand for it.
Most parties seem to value the profit
obtained from foliage over its healing powers.

---

*La Florida, 26 Feb. 1789, My dearest sister, I have clearly won the affection
of my lady. She knows of how I helped her. The life inside of her grows
steadily and she barely hides it under her silk mantua. Please feel comfort in
how I am adjusting to this new home. Without my lady and Valencio and
Chenoa my heart would be lost. I still miss you and our madre and padre*

and our seven little sisters. Only it is a little better now. Spring has arrived. The herbs flourish. I discover a new one each day and Chenoa helps me understand them. I fear my abandoned fields will be taken over by men to grow indigo. There is great demand for it. Most parties seem to value the profit obtained from foliage over its healing powers.

Let me pray now in anticipation of a Lenten transformation both here and in your life my sister.

Your beloved sister,

Lucia

Let me pray now in anticipation of a Lenten transformation both here and in your life my sister. Your beloved sister, Lucia

Prompted to search for more information about the medicinal plants and practices in the early South, Jewell dove into the other history books surrounding her.

She heard the bedroom door open. She expected Lydia. It was Christian. She glanced at the bedside clock. "Oh goodness. I lost track of the time. Are the kids okay?"

"Yep, making shapes with putty on the counter."

"I should go down."

"Hang on." Christian sat on the bed and placed his hand in hers. He didn't flash her his usual grin.

"What is it?" she asked, hesitantly.

He blew air through his nose and lifted his right hand, revealing a tri-fold paper. "Here." He handed it to Jewell.

She unfolded it and read. "What!" She jumped out of bed and paced. "She's suing for full custody? You have GOT to be kidding me."

"I wish I was."

Jewell's visual field narrowed. She imagined a hole opening in the floor and swallowing her. "Why did you have to contact her? We were happy." She paced, still clutching the document. She ran her hands through her hair, her face burned and smeared with tears. She whispered, "I can't lose him, I can't lose him, I can't lose him." She stopped and turned to Christian. "Did you confront her about the plant and the glitter?"

"I had to!"

"You shouldn't have stirred the beast in the first place. This is all your fault." She threw the document at him and stormed downstairs, unsure what to do or where to go.

"Jewell," Lydia called as she flew past her and the kids. "Where are you going?"

She grabbed Lydia's keys and called for Romeo. "I'll be back."

She drove to the beach with the top of the Beetle down. Romeo stuck his snout out of the carrier Jewell had grabbed from the SUV. She didn't think to bring his leash, though, so they just drove until enough salt air filled her lungs to calm her. She pulled over and sobbed out loud.

"Oh, Romeo. I'm such a horrible person. Christian may lose his son, Johnathan may have to go to a strange place with an evil stranger. Mom and Olivia would have a tremendous loss and all I thought of was myself."

She drove home defeated and sick to her stomach. When she entered the kitchen, she found Christian and Lydia at the kitchen counter. The kids lay on the living room floor playing. She went straight to Johnathan, knelt down and kissed the top of his head. She kissed him so many times she lost count. He giggled. Then she ran her fingers through Olivia's black curls, admiring her sweet face. She looked up from her play horse, "Mommy home."

"Yes, Mommy is home." She hesitantly turned to Christian and Lydia to see their concerned faces. She realized Christian must have filled Lydia in on the situation. "I'm so sorry, Christian. And sorry I took your car, Mom. That was disrespectful."

She turned and climbed the stairs. "C'mon, Romeo."

Before she could close the bedroom door behind her, Lydia pushed it open. "Wash your face and change your clothes. They're both soaked with tears. Then come back down for dinner."

"I can't, Mom."

"You can!"

"Did he tell you?"

"He did. While the kids were playing. It's certainly threatening and scary but she hasn't won yet and I doubt she will. Now, get ready and come downstairs. We all need to be together."

"No one needs me. I'm a horrible wife and mother."

"Fooey, you are not."

"Mom, what's wrong with me. Why can't I handle things like

everyone else?"

"I'd say, I'm responsible for that. I wasn't there to raise you." Lydia sagged against the door. "Let me help you now."

"No! You're all better off without me. Josh would have been better off without me. I'll stay up here and read."

"Jewell," Lydia pleaded.

Jewell slid out of her sandals, pulled the covers down and climbed into bed, still fully dressed. She kept the books scattered on the bed. "Up here, Romeo." He jumped onto the bed and lay on several books until she pulled them from under him.

Lydia shook her head. She left, shutting the door behind her. Jewell glanced at the closed door, and her heart sank. She located the marker and opened the book to Lucia's letters.

La Florida
14 April 1789

My dearest sister,

    It has been some time since my last letter and for this I am sorry. I use our herbs and practice our rituals. Still I am not with child. I am jaded.

    Where there could be two fathers there are none. God curses me for my sin. Mother Mary turns her head in shame.

    Easter has come and gone and I have no blessing.

    You should not be forced to read letters from such a person.

Your beloved sister,
Lucia

La Florida, 14 April 1789, My dearest sister, It has been some time since my last letter and for this I am sorry. I use our herbs and practice our rituals. Still I am not with child. I am jaded. Where there could be two fathers there are none. God curses me for my sin. Mother Mary turns her head in shame. Easter has come and gone and I have no blessing. You should not be forced to read letters from such a person. Your beloved sister, Lucia

La Florida
31 May 1789

My dearest sister,

It is with urgency I write this. Though I know you will not read the words urgently I still feel the need to write them.

We had a great celebration for important men from Madrid. They celebrated yet they speak of war. A war to come here in La Florida against the Americans and British and in our homeland against the British. I pray for my homeland and my familia.

My urgency comes from what happened during the celebration. They had us dance in our traditional way. There are eight of us who know it. The guitars players came with us, playing as we progressed through the streets.

There was much merriment however not all British and Americans accept our ways now. Some called for us to stop. The crowd rushed and I fell I could not find Valencio.

La Florida, 31 May 1789, My dearest sister, It is with urgency I write this. Though I know you will not read the words urgently, I still feel the need to write them. We had a great celebration for important men from Madrid.

They celebrated yet they speak of war. A war to come here in La Florida against the Americans and British and in our homeland against the British. I pray for my homeland and my familia. My urgency comes from what happened during the celebration. They had us dance in our traditional way. There are eight of us who know it. The guitar players came with us, playing as we progressed through the streets. There was much merriment; however, not all British and Americans accept our ways now. Some called for us to stop. The crowd rushed and I fell. I could not find Valencio.

One of the soldiers lifted me. My Lady visited my room. She told me Valencio had been cut. I know not how she knew of our association. I did not ask. I was grateful she told me. I gathered rags and water and rushed to the barn. He was there bleeding and holding his shirt against his stomach.

My sister we have the achillea plant here too. It is our same white flower and it grows well. I wet it and made a bandage of the rag. I made him tea with sage for the pain. He asked no questions.

He tells me I need to get away from my husband. He fears he directed someone into the crowd to stab him. He tells me once he heals he will take me to a new place called Georgia.

Pray for my true love as you know I pray for you always.

Your beloved sister,

Lucia

One of the soldiers lifted me. My lady visited my room. She told me *Valencio had been cut. I know not how she knew of our association. I did not ask. I was grateful she told me. I gathered rags and water and rushed to the barn. He was there bleeding and holding his shirt against his stomach. My sister, we have the achillea plant here too. It is our same white flower and it grows well. I wet it and made a bandage of the rag. I made him tea with sage for the pain. He asked no questions. He tells me I need to get away from my husband. He fears he directed someone into the crowd to stab him. He tells me once he heals he will take me to a new place called Georgia. Pray for my true love as you know I pray for you always. Your beloved sister, Lucia*

La Florida
6 June 1789

My dearest sister,

It is with great worry I write. Valencio has been given papers to return to Seville to fight against the British. I know my husband is behind this for the infantry is needed more here. Only two of the men are to return by ship this week. We have others secretly helping us so I can sneak onto the ship with him. My sister I may see you again after all. One day soon. I keep my letters short. I am sitting in the sun of the hayloft as Valencio sleeps. He needs to rest to heal enough for this great journey.

There is one more thing I tell you in confidence. I am with child and know it is Valencio's child growing within my womb. For my husband has not touched me for months and for this I am grateful.

Your beloved sister,
Lucia

La Florida, 6 June 1789, My dearest sister, It is with great worry I write. Valencio has been given papers to return to Seville to fight against the British. I know my husband is behind this for the infantry is needed more here. Only two of the men are to return by ship this week. We have others secretly helping us so I can sneak onto the ship with him. My sister, I may *see you again after all. One day soon. I keep my letters short. I am sitting in the sun of the hayloft as Valencio sleeps. He needs to rest to heal enough for this great journey. There is one more thing I tell you in confidence. I am with child and know it is Valencio's child growing within my womb. For my husband has not touched me for months and for this I am grateful. Your beloved sister, Lucia*

Jewell heard the door creak open. She wiped her tears and sat up in bed.

"I brought you a tray."

"Oh, maybe just a drink."

Later, she heard Christian snoring. Still wide awake, she stared at the ceiling.

The next morning Jewell awoke to the sound of water running in the shower. She dozed off and on until Christian stood in front of her dressed for work.

"I'm going to the University. Are you planning to rejoin the living today?"

"Humph." She rolled over, pulling the covers over most of her head. She heard the door close behind him.

Happy to reclaim her space, she sat up and flicked on the lamp next to her side of the bed. She spread her books out the way she liked and called for Romeo. He must have gone downstairs with Christian.

La Florida
10 June 1789

My dearest sister,

It is with great sorrow and worry that I write. We were tricked. Valencio and the other man were taken suddenly in the middle of the night and loaded onto a merchant ship instead of waiting for the military ship.

My evil husband must have heard of our plans for me to go with him. I have women who are working to help me get on another ship. Great works are underway. I promise.

My Lady must stay quiet but I know she's involved and powerful. She tells me often of her regret for bringing me here. It did little good as Spain is losing ground in La Florida.

Your beloved sister,
Lucia

La Florida, 10 June 1789, My dearest sister, It is with great sorrow and worry that I write. We were tricked. Valencio and the other man were taken suddenly in the middle of the night and loaded onto a merchant ship instead of waiting for the military ship. My evil husband must have heard of our plans for me to go with him. I have women who are working to help me get *on another ship. Great works are underway. I promise. My lady must stay quiet but I know she's involved and powerful. She tells me often of her regret for bringing me here. It did little good as Spain is losing ground in La Florida. Your beloved sister, Lucia*

La Florida
23 June 1789

Oh my dearest sister I know not when I will write to you again. I see little purpose.

Valencio and the other soldier were killed by a pirate attack on the ship. It is of suspicion to me that only the two were killed.

I live in fear —

Your beloved sister,
Lucia

La Florida, 13 June 1789, Oh my dearest sister, I know not when I will write to you again. I see little purpose. Valencio and the other soldier were killed by a pirate attack on the ship. It is of suspicion to me that only the two were killed. I live in fear. Your beloved sister, Lucia

Jewell's mouth fell open. She contemplated how to retrieve the laptop from the upstairs office without Lydia noticing and bugging her to get 'back among the living' as Christian put it. She imagined the two clustered in a corner analyzing and conspiring.

She cracked the door open and heard Lydia and the kids downstairs. She sneaked to the office and returned to her room with the laptop, prepared to delve into the history of the ship and Valencio's death.

One click of the mouse led to another until she spent hours from one spiraling information quest to the next. She read intently about the construction of eighteenth century ships, then wondered how she had headed down that path.

A knock at the door broke her concentration.

"Yes?"

"It's Mom. I have soup and tea."

"I'm not hungry."

"Well." Lydia opened the door. "There's something else."

"What?"

"I spotted something in the driveway. I went out to check, and it's a padded envelope with your name on it."

"Don't open it!"

"No." Lydia shook her head rapidly. "I didn't touch it. I called Christian and Detective Mary."

Jewell pulled herself together enough to go downstairs.

Christian arrived with Marc.

"Mary's still in the garage," Lydia informed them. "I'll take the kids to play in the backyard."

Mary must have opened the envelope in the garage. She entered the house wearing gloves and held her right hand out in a turned up fist. "I think it's okay."

"What is it?" Christian asked.

"A locket."

"A locket? As in a necklace?" Jewell asked.

"Yes, I can take it to my office and store it as evidence."

"Can I see it?" Jewell asked.

"I don't know if you want to."

She looked to Christian. "I do. I want to see it."

Mary opened the silver heart to reveal a photo of Romeo on the left and Maya on the right.

Jewell jumped back. "The pictures are from right here. From our backyard. Get Mom and the kids back in here."

"Now this has gone far enough," Christian said. "Threatening our pets. Plus, that ridiculous plant could have injured one of the kids."

"It's Elizabeth!" Jewell insisted.

"I agree now," Christian relented. "She didn't like me standing up to her. But I can't wrap my head around why she would've taken a chance on exposing Johnathan to a dangerous plant?"

"Because she doesn't care about anyone but herself and what she wants," Jewell yelled. "Becca has upgraded her diagnosis to a sociopath."

"You're right. I'm getting Lydia and the kids back in here." Christian headed for the glass doors.

"Any leads?" Marc asked.

"No. Whoever is sending these is covering up their tracks," Mary replied.

"How many times do I have to tell you? It's Elizabeth."

"I can't question her without probable cause, Jewell."

"Isn't suing us for custody now probable cause?"

"No, it isn't. I need something linking her to the deliveries. I have the envelope, but they attached your name with a typed label. I'll try to trace it, but I have a feeling it will come up empty. If it is her, we'll need more evidence before we can bring her in."

"Any idea who bought the plant from Travis?" Christian rejoined them having directed Lydia and the kids back in. "Did the delivery service know anything?"

"No, someone dropped it off at the delivery express warehouse. They said they have customers in and out all day. Their records only show a plant to be delivered to Jewell Caldwell at this address. The delivery fee paid in cash. I checked their tapes. The video isn't very clear. I didn't even see anyone carrying in a plant. Could be they had it in a box. There wasn't anyone on tape fitting Travis' description of the woman or anyone matching your picture of Elizabeth. Could be the suspect got someone else to do that part."

"Paying all these people. Wouldn't someone tell?"

Mary clucked her tongue. "You'd be surprised what people will do for a buck."

Days passed with Jewell self-secluded in her bedroom. She lost track of how many. No word from Mary.

Hunger and thirst forced her to accept a few of Lydia and Christian's trays. She spent most of her hours reading or sleeping. She became obsessed about Romeo and Maya's whereabouts. She kept them in her room other than the brief walks she allotted Romeo with Christian and Lydia. Maya sat on the windowsill, gazing outside and meowing.

She picked up reading the letters again and noticed Lucia had switched from writing to her sister and was now writing to her dead lover.

La Florida
15 June 1789

My dearest love Valencio,

I stay here in the barn all day. I go to the mansion only to sleep. I eat and drink only for our child's sake. He is what keeps me going on. I am sure it is your son I carry. Chenoa and I performed a test. He is healthy too.

Oh my love I cannot believe I lost you. Now I must stay here Married to your murderer.

Your beloved,
Lucia

La Florida, 15 June 1789, My dearest love, Valencio, I stay here in the barn

all day. I go to the mansion only to sleep. I eat and drink only for our child's
sake. He is what keeps me going on. I am sure it is your son I carry. Chenoa
and I performed a test. He is healthy too.
Oh my love, I cannot believe I lost you. Now I must stay here married to
your murder. Your beloved, Lucia

La Florida
16 June 1789

My dearest love Valencio;

I dream of us on our way to your Georgia. Oh would that it were so. One day runs into another here. The only thing to keep me going is your son. Sometimes I think I will walk out into the ocean and be swept away to join you.

Your beloved,
Lucia

La Florida, 16 June 1789, My dearest love, Valencio, I dream of us on our way to your Georgia. Oh would that it were so. One day runs into another here. The only thing to keep me going is your son. Sometimes I think I will walk out into the ocean and be swept away to join you. Your beloved, Lucia

Jewell heard a tap on the door. "I'm not hungry," she called out.

"Tough shit!" Becca opened the door.

Jewell sat wrapped in blankets with books spread over the bed scattered with used tissues among them. With eyes stinging from tearful bouts, she glanced at her friend.

"Whatchya got goin' on there?"

"Research."

"I see." Becca sat on the bed. "You realize you live in Florida, right?"

"I don't care. I'm cold." She pulled her blankets tighter.

"You're reading Lucia's letters?"

Jewell straightened herself to a more upright position in bed. Her flat expression turned bright as she caught Becca up to speed on Lucia's adventures and her other historical discoveries.

"I think we'll be ready for the seance," Jewell said. "The poor woman was distraught."

"Hmm, you don't say. That's great and all, but you know you have a family downstairs waiting for you to rejoin them. The kids are eating pulled chicken and mashed sweet potatoes. Olivia said, 'Hi, Aunt Behbeh' with a mouthful of orange goo."

"Aw, she did?" Jewell's face softened.

"Do you know how many people would give their eyeteeth for a family like yours?"

"Maybe someone who's a good mother."

"What are you talking about? You're an exceptional mother."

"I am not. They hate me."

"They love you."

"Johnathan won't listen. He said, and I quote, 'I hate you, Mommy.'"

"Every kid in the history of mankind has said that to their mother at one time or another. Didn't you find that in your history books there? Was there any discipline involved prior to his declaration?"

"Well…yeah."

"Uh-huh, I figured as much."

"See, why do you and everyone else in the world know all these basic things about life and I don't? I can't do it. This is what I do." Jewell picked up two books for emphasis. "I can throw myself into studies and research from one end of the galactic circle to the next. I know how to do this. I don't know how to do life. I watch you, I watch Christian. You know how to do life."

She felt another crying jag coming on and took quick deep breaths. "What's wrong with me?"

"Nothing's wrong with you. You just didn't have a stable childhood or a consistent role model."

Jewell let go and sobbed uncontrollably.

Becca moved closer. "What is it?"

"I don't know." She threw her hands down onto her lap full of tissues. "I mean we have the whole Elizabeth issue, but we'll win. I don't know, I'm just so emotional these days. I read Lucia's letters and I bawl. She's a stranger and I cry over her stories. I watch a movie and I bawl. Someone says boo to me and I bawl."

Becca's gaze turned into an intent stare.

"What?"

"Jewell, I know your periods are irregular, but when was your last one?"

"I don't know. I'm on the pill, but sometimes it doesn't start when

I finish the pack. My doctor told me if it doesn't come on, just start the new pack in seven days. But...well to be honest"–she twisted her mouth–"sometimes I forget when the seven days are up."

"Jewell, aren't you a scientist?"

"I am, but with not working, I don't follow a calendar as much."

"I mean do you hear yourself? You don't know when your last period was, you sometimes don't start your birth control on time, and you're uncharacteristically emotional."

Jewell stared, studying Becca's face until her words sunk in. Once they did, she gasped. "Oh!"

"Yep, that's what I'm thinking." Becca nodded slowly. "I'll go to the drugstore. You stay here. I won't tell anyone what I'm going for."

"Okay." A smile sneaked over Jewell's face, a smile she hadn't felt for days. She stopped crying, pulled back the covers and dangled her feet over the side of the bed.

"Hurry back."

Becca returned with a small bag bursting at the seams like an overstuffed pillow.

"How many tests do you think I need?"

"Well, what if you make a mistake?"

"Make a mistake? Peeing on a stick?"

Becca laughed. "I don't know, I'm excited. I might be an aunt again. Only, on my way back, it dawned on me, I shouldn't be the first one to know. Christian should be. I'm going downstairs to wait."

"Okay. I'll come down after the test."

She went into the bathroom and opened the package. She removed the cap and followed the instructions to perform the test. The color appeared immediately. She went downstairs in a daze.

"Hey, sweetheart." Christian rushed to guide her to the table. "Are you feeling better?"

"Let's get you some food," Lydia said, maneuvering to stand.

"No, I need to see Christian. Alone. Up in the bedroom."

"Mommy, I have a cupcake." Olivia smiled with pink icing on her lips, cheeks and somehow in her hair.

"I see that, sweetheart. I'll come right back to see you and J.J. in a few minutes."

Christian narrowed his eyes and tilted his head.

"It's okay. I just need to see you upstairs."

She watched Lydia shoot Becca an inquisitive glance. Becca shook her head, twirling her finger next to her ear.

They made it to the bed and Jewell pushed the books out of the way. Christian watched as she moved the heap of books.

"You've really been at it, haven't you?"

She glanced back at the pile. "Oh, I guess I have."

She patted the spot next to her on the bed and watched her husband hesitantly sit where she directed. She took both of Christian's hands into her own.

"You're scaring me, Jewell. Is everything okay? You haven't been yourself lately. Now this."

"No, I haven't. Been myself, that is. Um, Becca and I got to talking, and she went to the drugstore to get me something."

Jewell opened the top drawer where she had stuck the home pregnancy test with the cap covering the results.

"Is that…"

"Yes." She pulled the cap off. "And it's positive!" She threw her arms in the air.

Christian caught her up in a hug so tight, she could barely breathe. "Oh, babe. This is fantastic. It's the best news ever."

"You're happy?" Jewell asked.

"Happy? I'm ecstatic. What about you?"

She bobbed her head fervently. "I am." Tears streamed.

"Let's go tell everyone. Wait, does Becca know?"

"No, she went downstairs before I took the test. She wanted you to be the first to know."

"Brilliant."

"Wait, Christian. I have one important question."

"Uh-oh, what?"

"Will the baby speak English or British?"

"Ha-ha, you're still the comedian. Now, let's go downstairs and tell everyone our fabulous news."

"Hang on." Jewell contemplated. "What if we hold this just between us for tonight? Our own special space."

"I love it. But, you know they're down there wondering why you called me up here. And I'm sure Becca is about to jump out of her skin."

"True. Okay, you go down first and let me regroup. I'm afraid I'll give it away if I go down with you all happy. I've been down in the dumps an—"

"Gee, do you think?"

"I know I have been. I'm sorry. I refuse to let Elizabeth and her threats ruin our news. But, if I go downstairs beaming with joy, they'll be suspicious."

"Excellent point. When do you want to tell them?"

"Let's invite Becca over for breakfast around eight tomorrow and we'll make our announcement then. Should we invite your folks?"

Christian rubbed his chin. "No, that would be too obvious. We'll pop in to see them when I finish work."

"Splendid. Now you go ahead of me and give me time to practice my sullen face."

He stood to walk to the door, but instead rushed back and kissed her passionately.

Jewell went downstairs happy to see her family again. Becca stood with pleading eyes.

"Do you want to eat with me Becca? I finally feel a little hungry."

"Okay." Becca answered through a clenched jaw.

"I'll reheat dinner," Christian said.

"That's sweet," Jewell said.

"Yeah, real sweet." Becca pulled on Jewell's sleeve as they progressed to the kitchen table. She whispered, "Well?"

"Shh."

"But, Jewell."

"Come to breakfast tomorrow," Jewell whispered as they sat. "Eight a.m."

"What? And wait a whole night?"

Jewell spoke louder for all to hear. "Mom, Becca has a research project she needs help with. She'll come to breakfast tomorrow."

"Okay." Olivia went about tidying up toys on the living room floor.

"Wait a minute," Becca began as Christian delivered two plates. "If you want me to come for breakfast..."

"Hush," Jewell said.

"Yeah, hush," Christian reinforced.

Jewell held back her enthusiasm and picked at her plate of food, despite her urge to devour it in a matter of seconds.

Lydia came to sit with them at the table. "Becca is a natural counselor. Whatever she said to you worked miracles."

"She just made me realize what's important and how much I have." Jewell smiled at Becca.

Becca beamed back proudly.

When they retired to the bedroom for the night, Jewell realized she needed to release Maya from captivity. She let her out the bedroom door. The cat bolted. Jewell called to her, "But you're not going outdoors anytime soon."

Jewell cuddled with Christian as they talked excitedly about the baby.

When Christian quit responding, Jewell raised herself to see he was sleeping. Too excited to sleep, she dove back into the book and read

171

Lucia's final letter to Valencio.

Nine

Chapter 9

~∾ᘔᙣᘔᙣ∾~

The next morning Jewell awoke and found Christian's side of the bed empty. She stuffed the book with Lucia's letters into her backpack and flew down the steps. She saw Christian gathered with the kids, Lydia, and Becca. She also noted dishes covered with foil.

"I've got to go," she announced. "C'mon, Becca, come with me."

"What!" Christian exclaimed.

"I read Lucia's last letter. I know who the ghost is."

"Jewell!" Christian said, his eyes pleading.

"Sorry, I have to do this. I texted Sherry to bring her camera. We're heading to the mansion."

Christian followed them outside. "What about our plans to tell everyone this morning?"

"Yeah." Becca folded her arms across her chest. "You kept me waiting all night."

"I know and I still want to. Only, why don't we take everyone out to a relaxing dinner tonight and tell them? Can you go, Becca?"

"I can." Becca grinned then performed a churn the butter dance. "I guess I know your test results if we're going out to dinner." She sang the words as she took the dance move into a circle.

"Quiet, no tipping off anyone else," Jewell said. "We'll tell them over dinner. Practice acting surprised, Becca. We can share a nice bottle of wine—oh, wait, I guess I can't have any wine."

"No, absolutely not—", "No—"

"Okay, sorry, you two. It's just sinking in." Jewell smiled and rubbed her lower belly, then kissed Christian.

"I promise, we'll make it special tonight. Invite Caroline and Roger. Have Lydia invite George. Sorry, this mansion thing is something I have to do."

"All right, I'll make the reservations," Christian conceded. "Want to go to Gil's place?"

"Perfect. I could eat a whole lasagna myself. I love you." She and Becca rushed to the SUV.

"Oh, and one more thing, Christian," she called back as she neared the vehicle.

"What?"

"We're gonna fight that psycho from England. And WIN!"

She drove with Becca to the outer perimeter as close as possible to the mansion. They ran to meet Sherry and ended up beating her there. The mansion was open with no patrons.

"Are you going to reveal who the ghost is?"

"You'll see soon enough. Haven't you gotten enough news this morning?" Jewell nudged Becca with her elbow.

They approached the welcome counter.

"Hi, I'm Jewell Harrington," she addressed the man seated behind the counter. "This is my friend, Becca. We are part of Seana's group trying to identify the ghost."

"You can see"—the man swept his arm to direct their attention around the place—"we don't exactly have much going on here at the moment."

"Has the haunting stopped?"

"Oh, gracious me, no. It's the visitors who've stopped, not the ghost. I'm the only one on staff at the moment."

"So, the haunting is still going on." She turned to Becca.

"That it is," he said, "but I don't pay it much mind."

Sherry entered breathlessly, her camera case in hand.

"Have you noticed any particular area being haunted more than others?"

"Yes ma'am, the basement and the ballroom. Odd combination, don't ya think?"

"Maybe not," Jewell said. "Can we go anywhere we wish?"

"Lady, you three have the run of the place as far as I'm concerned. I'm going to stay right here and read my book."

Jewell headed for the basement stairs. She turned back to see Becca and Sherry frozen.

"I-I don't know, Jewell."

"Yeah, me neither."

"C'mon. It'll be fine."

"Yeah, go on. I patrol the entire place a couple times a day. It don't scare me none."

"Okay." Sherry took tiny steps toward Jewell.

Becca shrugged and joined them.

"Wait," Jewell said. "Let me see your camera."

Sherry removed it from the case and handed it to Jewell.

"How do I set the shutter to silent?"

Sherry pushed some buttons. "There."

They descended to the bottom floor, and Jewell experienced the familiar chill and raised hairs.

"This is creepy, Jewell," Sherry said. "And too quiet."

"I'm glad it's quiet. That's better than moans or rattling pipes," Becca said.

"Ew, did you have to say that?" Sherry shivered. "Where are we headed, anyway?"

"Back to the bedroom at the end of the hall. Where Lucia stayed and her whereabouts were last known."

Sherry drew in a quick breath and stopped.

"Come on. You've made it this far." Jewell whipped her arm to motion her forward. "But come quietly. No sounds, even from your shoes." She pointed to their feet.

The three approached the door, and Jewell held her hand out for them to stop. She reached for Sherry's camera, then from outside the room she set the camera to zoom, aimed it toward the mirror and snapped the silent shutter repeatedly.

When she finished, she stepped back with the others and began advancing the images. A vase dropped to the floor and rolled around. It didn't break.

The three jumped. Becca and Sherry turned to run.

"No, hang on. I see something." Jewell stood advancing the shots.

They gathered around.

"Ah!" Sherry cried. "It's a man!"

"A horrible angry looking man," Becca added.

"Let's go!" Jewell screeched. "It's just as I suspected." They dashed for the steps. Jewell felt a force like a powerful gust of wind push her backward, almost throwing her off balance. She reached for Becca, who heaved her up the steps.

"What was that?" Sherry asked.

"Yeah, Jewell, I could hardly pull you."

"It was Lucia's murderer." Jewell stood bent at the waist with her hands on her thighs.

Breathlessly they approached the man who cooly glanced up from his book.

"We know. We know who it is," Jewell said, still working on composure. "We know who's haunting the mansion."

"Great. Now can you get rid of it so we can get back to normal operations?" The man resumed reading his book.

All thirteen women who had gathered for the initial mansion tour rose to the emergency call to Rhita's. They pulled four tables together.

Jewell passed Sherry's camera throughout the group. The unnerving image flooding the screen.

"Ah!" Candi pressed two fingers to her mouth.

"He looks so hateful." Gabby passed it quickly to Z.

"You're not a-kiddin'," Z said.

Nicci glimpsed the screen, then passed the camera to Della Rae without commenting.

"How did you figure it out, Jewell?" Maggie asked.

She provided a synopsis of Lucia's letters, then read the final one out loud to the group.

La Florida
18 June 1789

My dearest love Valencio,

The wicked man knows. He admitted he arranged for your murder. He had been following us. He knows I carry your child. I threatened to turn him in. We argued in my room. I went to leave and he slammed the door to keep me inside.

None of the staff would stop him. They all live in fear of him. He held the door shut and came close to my face. He told me to go ahead and report that he had these two men killed. You because you were my lover and the other man to avert suspicion and make it look [like how he says] random.

He says to go ahead and tell and he will tell that I am an adulterer

La Florida, 18 June 1789, My dearest love, Valencio, The wicked man knows. He admitted he arranged for your murder. He had been following us. He knows I carry your child. I threatened to turn him in. We argued in my room. I went to leave and he slammed the door to keep me inside. None of the staff would stop him. They all live in fear of him. He held the door shut and came close to my face. He told me to go ahead and report that he had these two men killed. You because you were my lover, and the other man to avert suspicion and make it look [like how he says] random. He says to go ahead and tell and he will tell that I am an adulterer...

and even more dangerous tell everyone
that I am a witch.

I must stay quiet for our child's sake.
I will be jailed if I am called an adulterer
and hanged if I am called a witch.
I sit here in the barn writing to you.
Only I must go back to the mansion
tonight. I have no choice.

Your beloved forever,
Lucia

...and even more dangerous, tell everyone that I am a witch. I must stay quiet for our child's sake. I will be jailed if I am called an adulterer and hanged if I am called a witch. I sit here in the barn writing to you. Only I must go back to the mansion tonight. I have no choice. Your beloved forever,

Lucia

Then she passed the book around for each to read the first paragraph in Professor Cheryl Cummings closing words.

The conclusion:

An anonymous report made on June 19, 1789, told of Floriana Lucia Ramos y Montoya's disappearance. The report showed she was last seen on June 18, 1789 by mansion staff, which correlates with the date of her last letter. The Spanish authorities held an interview with General Zia y Velarde. Documented suspicion of his guilt exists, but with no body or murder weapon, the authorities filed the case as unsolved.

Z read the conclusion first. "That poor woman."

She handed the book to Gabby. "Yeah, no one knows what happened to her. That's so sad."

"And her poor unborn baby." Candi shook her head and passed it to Nicci.

"Now, this part is actual history and interesting," Nicci said. "I'd like to borrow this book, Jewell."

"Sure, Nicci. Just take it back to the library before the due date. I think I'll check it out again when you return it. I'd like to read the stories a second time."

Seana studied the words intently, then closed her eyes and placed a flat palm over the open book.

Once Sherry read it, she turned her lips down and offered the book to Della Rae.

"What do we do now?" Della Rae asked Seana, then continued to pass the book.

"You all do nothing," Seana responded. "A spirit of this nature requires an exorcism. The priest and I will take this task on. I'm calling right now to have the mansion vacated until we can perform the ritual. No one should go in there."

"You ain't just whistlin' dixie, sister." Della Rae nodded at Seana for emphasis. "We don't need to touch that mess with a ten-foot pole."

Jewell's eyes widened as she thought about the danger she just escaped. She promised herself to never again put herself or her baby in jeopardy.

"I'm fine with staying away." Z waved her hands.

"I don't know," Gabby said. "Isn't it…well…kinda anticlimactic? I mean no seance for closure."

"True," Maggie agreed. "There was some satisfaction in knowing we sent Clara on to her next destination."

"Trust me," Jewell said. "I came too close to this spirit, and he was terrifying. His hostility was palpable, even from the dead." As far as missing a seance, Jewell didn't feel cheated. She felt connected to Lucia and her stories. "Hey, I have an idea. When Nicci has read it, why don't each of you check it out from the library? It will help you feel closer to the story."

"Great idea," Becca said. "And didn't you tell me the University houses her original letters?"

"I did!"

"Field trip, field trip," Z chanted.

Bella Cibo's was turning out to be the family's favorite Southbridge restaurant.

Once seated, drinks ordered, and bread delivered, Lydia asked what occasion had sparked such a special dinner in the middle of the week.

Christian and Jewell exchanged knowing glances. A place deep inside of Jewell wanted to keep this secret between the two of them.

Christian took Jewell's hands. "Do you want to? Or do you want me to?"

Lydia shifted her eyes from George to Becca to Christian's parents.

"I will." Jewell smiled and glanced about the table. "We're going to have a baby."

"Oh, my heart!" Lydia threw her arms in the air. She leaped from her chair to hug Christian and Jewell.

Caroline and Roger followed close behind.

"Say…did you know?" Lydia looked suspiciously at Becca.

"Me? Feh." She swiped her hand through the air.

Jewell turned her attention to Johnathan and Olivia. Christian had gotten out of his seat and knelt between them. Jewell joined him in a crouched position.

"Do you understand, baby?" She asked Johnathan.

"Uh-huh. We're going to have another Olivia."

"Or another J.J.," Christian said.

"Actually," Jewell said. "There could never be another Olivia or J.J."

Christian put his arm around her and kissed the top of her head.

"Mommy's right. A brother or sister."

Olivia appeared unfazed as she sat drinking milk from her tippy cup. She turned her head from side to side, enthralled with the red glow of the restaurant.

"I say we have a toast," George said and beckoned Gil. "Please, Gil, may we have a bottle of Mionetto Prosecco and"—George counted around the table—" five glasses? And four glasses of sparkling cider."

"Oh course. My pleasure."

The excitement of the news settled, and the conversation turned to George. He filled the group in on his life. How his wife of twenty-five years had died over four years ago and how his only daughter, Jennifer, lives in Southbridge. He passed his phone to show off pictures of his twin grandsons. "They're eleven now." A smile lit his face.

As the waiter served the food, Jewell leaned toward Caroline. "Any news on you know who?"

"No, I can barely stand to look at her with what she's putting you and Christian through. I know I should try to meet with her to keep up with her schemes. I just can't bring myself to talk to her anymore. I do still talk to her mother, though. Her mother met a man and moved up North. She hasn't visited Johnathan for some time, but she used to see him and bring birthday and Christmas gifts. Only, she hasn't been around for a while. I don't know." Caroline shook her head. "I don't get people."

"Hmm, Christian has never mentioned her."

"I can see why. She's been absent. As a grandmother, I don't see how she stays away no matter how far the distance. At least she's a source of information for me. She's furious with Elizabeth about this ridiculous lawsuit and her, well, suspected extra-curricular activities."

Jewell stared ahead. She felt the lines in her forehead wrinkle. "Caroline, why don't you come to the house for lunch again tomorrow. We'll put our heads together."

"I like the sound of that." Caroline clinked her glass to Jewell's.

Jewell held up her clear glass with sparkling cider. "My, how the times have changed."

Lydia made her famous chicken salad for lunch. The kind Jewell loved with grapes and walnuts. They set up the play table again for the kids in the living room.

"Do you have an inkling if the baby is a girl or a boy, Jewell?" Caroline claimed her seat at the kitchen table.

"No, not really. I'm just getting used to the fact that a life's growing inside me." Jewell sat next to her mother-in-law.

"Your smile makes your face glow." Caroline took her hand. "I could have sworn Christian was a girl when I carried him. Named him, Christina, in my mind. That tells you how much I know."

"The book I read recently mentioned an ancient practice to reveal gender. Maybe I'll look into it."

"It doesn't really matter, Jewell." Lydia slid a bowl heaping with her chicken salad onto the table along with slices of multigrain breads and rolls. "You kids have those high-tech scans these days. You'll know the gender in about six weeks from now. That is, if you wish to know." Lydia leaned her ear toward Jewell as if awaiting an answer.

Jewell played dumb, pretending to focus on pouring sweet tea.

"Well, Jewell?" Lydia finally asked.

"Yes. We'll want to know." She paused. "Oh my goodness, now you've got all kinds of gender reveal party ideas bombarding my mind."

"There you go. My girl's back." Lydia smiled.

"Now on a more serious note." Jewell cut a diagonal line through her sandwich chock-full of chicken salad, lettuce leaves and tomato. "How can we get Elizabeth back to England? Honestly, if she would have been genuinely interested in Johnathan's well-being, I would have been the first to encourage visits. But, I think we can all agree, that is not her motive. Doesn't anyone else think it's odd she jumps straight to custody and never even asked to visit with him? I can't imagine being away from him all these years. Not questioning what he's doing, how he is, how he's growing." Jewell felt immediate remorse, realizing what her words must mean to Lydia, who left her and Nathanael. Jewell quickly glanced at her mother, biting her lip.

Lydia smiled, shook her head and waved a dismissive hand through the air.

"Exactly," Caroline agreed. "I can't imagine she wants him full time. Like I said, I've known this girl since middle school. She's self-centered. And thanks to you and Becca, we have a diagnosis."

"So what's going on?" Jewell looked between Lydia and Caroline. "We're all intelligent women here. We can figure this out."

"I don't know. I wish I knew, Jewell." Caroline sipped her sweet tea. "You know, I grew up with proper tea in the afternoon, but I have to admit the sweet tea around here is the bee's knees."

Jewell sighed with her mouth full of sandwich. Her mind raced a hundred miles an hour. She placed two fingers over her mouth and swallowed hard. "What do you think is motivating this sudden disruption?"

"Well." Caroline shook her head and looked from Lydia to Jewell. "I can tell you this. She was always mighty jealous of Christian."

"Yeah, like you said, keeping him away from his friends in school?" Jewell pushed her plate away and leaned back in the chair.

"But there was one specific incident. They were on this break." Caroline made air quotes.

"Really? What happened?"

"He started seeing a cute little girl. Really sweet. Not glamorous like Elizabeth, mind you, but much nicer. Not that Elizabeth was nice at all. Roger and I were relieved that she was out of the picture. We liked Elizabeth's parents. This was before their divorce. Still, it was nice to see Christian with a girl who treated him right."

"I'm sure. Did he stay with this new girl for long?" Jewell rested her chin on her hands and leaned toward Caroline. Lydia followed suit.

"Oh, heavens no. Elizabeth wasn't about to let him be happy with anyone else. It was her or no one."

"Yet, after she married him, and had his son," Jewell clarified, "she took off for another continent. A whole ocean away from Christian and her son. Now, who can figure that out?"

"That's just it. I think she liked the thought of Christian dedicated to Johnathan and not with any other woman. In fact, it was that way for quite a while. Until she came back for a brief period."

"Yeah, Christian told me they gave the marriage a second try."

"They did, and I was hopeful because it was soon after my mother died. Christian was so close to her. When my father died, she moved from England to Southbridge and lived with us. Christian and his grandmama were inseparable. So, when Elizabeth came back after her death, it comforted me at first, until I watched her grow restless. I figured what was to follow."

"She left again," Lydia said.

"Yes, she did."

"She's a selfish, awful person." Jewell folded her arms.

"I agree," Caroline said. "Part of me thought the money would keep her around."

"The money?" Lydia asked.

"Christian and Johnathan's inheritance," Jewell said. "He doesn't talk about it. He told me briefly when we attended marriage classes at our church."

When they finished eating, Caroline kissed the kids goodbye and Jewell accompanied her to her car. "You've been helpful, Caroline. Thanks."

"I have, dear? I don't see how."

Jewell pulled into an empty public parking spot at the beach. There were plenty of open spots this time of year. When she stepped out of the SUV and flung the door closed, her dusty rose swing skirt blew up around her waist. She quickly caught the hem and forced it back down over her thighs as she peered around to make sure no one had been watching.

She gathered her hair and swept it over her right shoulder, juggling her phone, a purse and an oversize paper bag. Then she checked the settings on her phone, slipped it into her clutch purse and tucked it under her left arm. Still holding the paper bag in her left hand, she used both hands for holding her skirt in place. With all her painstaking planning to get her outfit just right, she hadn't factored in the ocean wind. She hoped it wasn't a sign of how the encounter was about to play out.

When she reached the sand, she braved letting go of her skirt with her right hand and used it to shield her eyes from the sun. It was so bright she had to squint through her sunglasses to make out the objects closer to the water. Then she spotted her. Ms. Perfect wore a bodycon dress—the only style that wouldn't blow about recklessly. And she had braided her chestnut locks into one long rope.

Jewell breathed in the salt air, said a silent prayer, then headed toward Elizabeth.

"What's this all about?" Her icy tone pierced Jewell. "It's not wise for us to meet."

"I know. I appreciate you hearing me out. As I specified over the phone, I believe I have a solution that will get us both what we want."

"Yes?"

Jewell knew if she could see the woman's eyes through her dark lenses, they'd have just rolled to the sky.

"Yes, you see," Jewell continued, "I've manipulated things to force my mother to move out and take Olivia with her. It's not like she's mine and Christian's. Now, the only one I need to clear out is Johnathan. And that's where you come in. Then I'll have Christian all to—"

"What are you talking about? Christian will never go for this. I know him. He'll be coming to England with Johnathan. You need to brace yourself for it."

A gust of wind whipped about them and Jewell struggled with whether to hold her skirt or her hair.

"No, trust me, he'll go for it. We had a honeymoon of epic proportions and ever since then, he'll do anything I want." Jewell enjoyed the sulk her words brought to Elizabeth's face. She knew she should feel guilty, but she didn't. "I've been playing up the kind of life we can have with no brats tying us down. You know, make love in the middle of the day. In any damn room we choose."

"I..I…"

"You what? I see you're doubtful. I promise I will make this happen. Johnathan will be yours and yours alone within weeks. I've been dropping hints and painting the picture of how it could be. I told him we could fly to Stratford quarterly to visit. He's warming up to the —"

"Now, see here. You have no rights. You have no say in this. You're the reason I'm forced to pursue this ridiculous custody case." She flailed her arms. "Coming in and seducing Christian. You can't tell me how things will be."

"You see, that's where you're wrong. What I've got in this bag here is why I can tell you how things will be. Unless you want to go to jail." Jewell offered the bag to Elizabeth who drew back but glimpsed the contents without accepting it.

"Here, they're your things. You sent them to me. I'm just returning them."

"They're not mine. I don't know what you're talking about."

Jewell dropped the bag at Elizabeth's feet then surrendered to the ocean's airstream and let her skirt and hair fly. "I have all the rights where Christian is concerned and I'm trying to help you have all the rights where his son is concerned. Let's be partners."

"Well, I never. I have no intention of being your partner. You just wait until I tell Christian what you are up to. He will be on a plane heading back home with me so fast your head will spin. We will leave you and your idiotic outfit"—she swept her hand in the air from Jewell's head to her toes—"behind. Ha!"

"You mean Christian and Johnathan will be on a plane with you."

"Whatever. Who cares if the kid comes. I can afford a full-time nanny to keep him out of our hair. Then it will be I who has the afternoon love making with Christian, not you."

"You don't say." Jewell felt her brightest smile sneak over her face.

"What are you grinning about? You are about to lose."

"Whatever you say. You know best. I'll just go home and pack their bags." Jewell turned and plodded through the sand toward her vehicle.

"Are you insane? Where are you going? Take these things."

Jewell continued to trek to the parking lot.

"I'm talking to you."

Elizabeth's voice faded into the background as Jewell neared the SUV. She hurried inside, pulled her cell phone out and hit 'play.' She danced in her seat as Elizabeth's words broadcasted loud and clear. She forwarded the recording to Elizabeth with the message: *Feel free to arrange your ticket for one to carry you back across the pond. This message just went to our lawyer.*

Jewell drove straight to the University and played the recording for Christian.

"Jewell, that was awfully risky."

"I know, but her already slim chance at custody just got a lot slimmer, or rather…nil."

"What was in the bag? Mary has all the evidence."

189

"Ha! I bought a plant and covered it in an opaque wrap, then placed it in a paper bag with an empty box and a padded envelope. I was hoping she'd take the bait and confess to sending them. But, even though we don't have a confession of her criminal activity, at least we have her own words declaring she has no interest in caring for Johnathan."

"How funny. The one who thinks herself so clever was outsmarted by my genius wife. Still, it's unbelievable that she still wants me."

"I don't think she really does. No offense."

He dropped his head.

"Very funny."

Christian smirked.

"No, I believe her primary motive was the inheritance. I know you only mentioned it to me once, but you said it was significant. I had forgotten about it until Caroline spoke of it at lunch. Plus, I think Elizabeth just doesn't want me, or anyone else for that matter, to have you. Part of the narcissistic personality disorder is to target a perceived enemy. She was ready to fight to the death until I threatened her freedom. I think way back when she left for the second time, she figured you'd do all the heavy lifting raising Johnathan then once grown, she could swoop back in? Only, my emergence on the scene kind of messed that up."

"Really? I get the money thing. What made you think she'd be jealous of me?"

"I got that idea from your mum too."

"Mum?"

"Yes, she told me a story about some girl from high school you went out with during a break from Elizabeth."

"Oh, Crystal."

"Still remember her name, ugh?" Jewell folded her arms tightly across her chest and pursed her lips. She hoped to see Christian squirm, but failed to hold her giggle in.

"You know you're the only one, babe." He moved in, erasing any distance. "Pretty dress."

"It's a skirt."

He kissed her before she had time to thank him for the compliment. "Do you think this is behind us?" He continued to hold Jewell close.

"I do. I bet she's booking a flight as we speak."

"You know, by the time our marriage had ended, for a second time, I knew she was shallow. I just never imagined her sinking this low."

"She sure put us through a lot of hell. Christian, I hated saying those awful things about our kids." She pouted. *"Our kids,"* she repeated with a raised voice.

Ten

Chapter 10

⚬ↄ૦ᒋↄↄ⌇

J ewell slid the social section of the newspaper to Lydia. "Here.
Read the excellent news."

"Oh, my." Lydia said. "The headline says it all. 'Halloween
Party Planned at Reopened Governor's Mansion.' Yippie!"

"Yep, seems they eradicated the ghost. It says the mansion has been
free of any suspicious happenings for a week. Let's hope it stays that
way."

"Are we going?" Lydia laid the newspaper on the table.

"I'd like to, wouldn't you?"

"I would. I'll talk to George about it."

"Great, and I'll talk to Christian."

"Speaking of whom." Lydia wiggled her index finger toward the
stairs.

"Hey, honey. What's up? You look serious."

"I don't mean to," Christian said. "Just letting it sink in."

"Letting what sink in?"

"That was Marc." Christian held up his cell phone.

"He just called?"

"Yes, only just. Elizabeth dropped the lawsuit. We're free."

"Well, that's marvelous news! Not surprising, but marvelous." Jewell leaped to her feet. "Why aren't you thrilled?"

"I am. Just a little shell-shocked."

"I get that, Christian," Lydia said. "Me too."

"I don't get it. I'm ready to dance and shout at the top of my lungs." Johnathan came into the kitchen with Olivia close behind.

"Mommy is happy," Johnathan said.

"Yes, Mommy is happy." She picked up Olivia and danced with Johnathan while humming the country tune she and Christian had two-stepped to in the kitchen of her tiny yellow house. The same smile that had tightened her cheeks that day, returned.

When the celebration and breakfast ended, Christian announced he was heading to work.

"Wait, you didn't say. What about going to the mansion next Saturday? For the Halloween party?"

"I don't see why not?"

"Perfect! I'll text the gang."

Check the Southbridge Times. The mansion is cleared and reopening!

Della Rae: *I saw that. Great work, Jewell.*

Jewell: *It was teamwork. My household is going, anyone else in?*

Sherry: *I'm in.*

Z: *Miranda and I are in and she said it's a costume party.*

Maggie: *It is and I have an idea.*

Z: *Hey, Maggie's texting.*

Maggie: *I am, because as I said, I have an idea.*

Nicci: *Just joined. What's your idea, Maggie?*

Maggie: *I haven't had time to fully develop it, but what if I get permission for a little performance during the festivities? A chance to showcase flamenco dancing.*

Candi: *Hey, Maggie is on here. But we don't know flamenco.*

Maggie: *Exactly, I didn't say it wouldn't be a challenge, but my wheels are turning. Who's in?*

Jewell: *I am.*

Becca: *I'm in. It sounds way cool.*

Z: *I'm there. Miranda wants to know if she can join in? Her mother used to dance flamenco.*

Maggie: *Really? Can her mother come to class on Wednesday?*

Z: *No can do. She lives in New Mexico.*

Della Rae: *Sounds exciting to me. Count me in.*

Nicci: *I guess I'm in.*

Gabby: *Wait, I just heard my phone. One of the boys must have stuffed it under a cushion. Let me catch up.*

Sherry: *I'm in for whatever we're doing.*

Lydia: *Lynn and I have been texting separately. It may be a silly question, but can we be included somehow?*

Jewell's head whipped towards Lydia, who granted a sheepish grin.

Maggie: *Give me a second to think, y'all.*

Gabby: *Just caught up. For sure, I'm in.*

Jewell: *Candi?*

Candi: *Oh, didn't I say? I'm in.*

Maggie: *For time's sake, I'll order the costumes. I get a wholesale and troupe discount so I'll keep it reasonable and text the cost once I've placed the order. Text me your sizes and bring payment on Wednesday.*

Della Rae: *Mine's down to a size 12.*

Maggie: *Congratulations, Della Rae. Y'all can email me your sizes separately though. I could probably guess, but just to be safe... And, Lydia and Lynn, we'll fit y'all in the dance somehow. I better get to the drawing board.*

Maggie: *Wait, one more thing, y'all better come an hour early, if possible. We'll need extra time.*

Jewell thought Wednesday would never roll around. She anxiously anticipated the flamenco costumes and dance. She parked in a public spot, then scurried alongside Lydia to the studio.

"I feel like a teenager," Lydia said.

"I'm so glad you and Lynn are joining in. And Miranda. I've never understood why she didn't dance with us, anyway."

"Maybe Z just wanted something for herself?"

As they neared the steps of the studio, Jewell paused.

"What is it?" Lydia asked, halting her steps too.

"Listen." The stirring, rhythmic pulse of a Spanish guitar struck Jewell's ears and whirled through her body. Dramatic pauses between the strident chords drawing her in more deeply than the melody itself, as the rests made room for the song's meaning to hover above. The breathy notes conjured images of Lucia with her head erect, chest proudly lifted and arms above her head forming the letter O; her posture unmistakably strong and yet soft at the same time.

"Jewell, it's only music. Aren't you used to music coming from the studio?"

"But, it's live." The sounds arising from the studio penetrated Jewell's soul with an energy recorded music lacked. This was happening now. It connected her to the artist as if frozen in time and space.

"Are you ready?" Lydia asked as Candi approached from the other side of the street.

"Hey, you two. What's up?"

"Maggie has apparently invited a guest," Jewell said. "Let's go in."

They entered the studio to witness Maggie, Nicci, Sherry and Della Rae swarming a seated guitar player. They dropped their belongings and joined the others.

When the man stopped playing, they clapped. He smiled.

Maggie addressed Jewell, Lydia and Candi as Becca and Lynn entered the studio. "Hang on, wait until they get over here with us."

Becca approached to stand next to Jewell and bumped hips with her. Lynn went to stand next to Lydia.

"I was fixin' to introduce Luis. He will give us a quick bio once everyone is here, but let me say, you can find him playing live throughout Southbridge at various restaurants on the weekends."

"That's fabulous," Lynn said. "Why haven't I ever heard you?"

"He plays at San Sebastian's," Maggie said. "Y'all need to get out more. Please, Luis, continue playing, if you'd like."

He began strumming again, adding intermittent taps on the guitar top that tempted Jewell to move her feet.

The rest of the class plus Miranda arrived. Even Gabby showed up on time for this special class.

"Okay, let's go over to the cushions. Everyone take a seat."

"Hey, I'll be fifty next month." Lynn lowered herself to sit on a floor cushion. "Someone might have to heave me up."

"Oh, Mom, stop. You're in great shape."

With everyone settled, Maggie introduced Luis.

He stood and approached the group with guitar in hand. He wore a white shirt with puffed sleeves and a black vest. He had combed his ebony hair back and Jewell guessed his age to be around forty.

"Let me warn you," Maggie said. "He's a man of few words."

Luis's eyes darted to the floor. "I feel it's best to let my music speak."

He laughed, and so did the group.

"I have been playing guitar since I was ten years old. My father and his father before him played. My guitar may look like any other, but is constructed differently. They design the wood to produce the snapping sound of percussion. See the plate for tapping?" He pointed out the clear plate covering the middle body of the guitar that Jewell wouldn't have noticed without looking closely. "This clamp at the top produces the higher pitch of flamenco music."

Maggie rowed both hands in the air as if encouraging more information. "See what I mean by a man of few words. Luis, tell us about flamenco here in Southbridge."

"Oh, yes." He chuckled. "I was born and raised here in Southbridge. Years ago, we had more flamenco dancers, as we say, bailaor, and singers, cantaor. But now, I often play by myself, not only in restaurants, but I travel to festivals. Maggie has my business cards. Now, I will play." He laughed again. "I almost forgot. And I am a tocador, a guitarist. I'll play a cante jondo, my favorite. It's not for beginners to dance to. The rhythms are complex, but it fits for when you lose a lover or experience a tragedy."

He sat again, crossed his legs to support the guitar and played. Jewell listened, immersed in his haunting tune.

When he stopped, they clapped. "Thank you, Luis. He has to leave for a gig. Let's show him some more appreciation."

They stood and clapped. Z whistled. Della Rae led a zaghareet bellydance call.

Once he gathered his things to leave, Maggie motioned for them to sit on the cushions again. She walked to her desk and retrieved a large booklet. Once she stood before them, Jewell could see it was a flip chart.

"Nina is a friend of mine who studies and dances flamenco. She could not attend tonight's class, but lent me her educational tool." Maggie flipped through the colorful pages explaining the history and art of flamenco. "Flamenco is not only a dance form, it comprises a culture. It's a language communicated through and between the musicians, singers and dancers then projected out to the audience. The nature of this art form is improvisation. They pass the lead among the performers. As one example, when a dancer wishes to speed the tempo, she taps in ever increasing velocity in a subida step. The musicians know to increase the tempo."

"As you can imagine," Maggie continued, "it would take many years to properly learn flamenco and do the art form justice. With that said, we will mimic the feel through a skirt dance." Maggie returned the flip chart to her desk and retrieved items draped over her desk chair.

"This is our costume." Maggie displayed a bright red skirt with a black ruffle hem in her right hand and a black crop top in her left.

The class uttered oohs and ahs.

They stood to inspect the items. Maggie flipped the top over to reveal criss-crossed straps in the back. "I think those of us with long hair ought to pull it up to show off the back, plus buns are in keeping with flamenco costuming. Now, your skirts are full. They're perfect for flaring when we spin and wide enough to serve as our dance prop in this number. You'll need black tights to wear under your skirts and the flat shoes we wore for the Fall Fest. I also suggest we purchase fresh red carnations for our hair. Cynthia's Flora creates hair pins out of fresh flowers. Please wear a shawl of your choice. We'll use those as our coverup. I don't feel it's necessary to cover our entire costumes given it's a costume party."

"Okay." Maggie stepped into her skirt, pulled it up over her yoga pants. She grabbed the bottom sides and lifted them to tuck into her waistband, creating a waterfall effect on both sides. She handed Della Rae the top. "Here, hold this for me."

"We will dance to recorded music, but I hope one day we can dance to Luis's guitar." She clicked the remote she had tucked in her bra and festive music played. She danced, posing in flamenco stances, then untucked the skirt from her sides and used it to make gorgeous sweeping shapes. The ruffles added to the beauty of the displays.

When the music stopped, the class cheered.

"Beautiful—" "Bravo—" "I love it—"

"See, no complicated moves. The skirts are so eye catching in their various formations, we need not dazzle with complicated moves. Plus, our posturing pays tribute to flamenco."

"I love it," Candi said.

"Me too," Becca said.

"What do you think your mother would say, Miranda?"

"I say she'd give a big stamp of approval."

"Now, y'all know you will have to practice this every day before the party." Maggie grabbed a stack of papers from her desk and passed them around. "Here's the order of the steps. I know how y'all like to get together. I think you should do so this week and next week to practice. We'll run through it again next Wednesday. Can you three attend?" She addressed Lydia, Lynn and Miranda.

The three confirmed they could attend the next class.

"What do you envision for us?" Lydia asked. "I know you said the moves are simple. Maybe for our girls, but I don't know about me spinning like that."

"I'm with Lydia," Lynn said.

"What about you, Miranda?" Maggie asked. "I think you could learn the skirt dance."

"Yeah, I think I could."

"Then, I've got Lynn and Lydia covered," Maggie said. "You two will be our bookends. I'll teach you a modified version of the postures. Y'all will rotate through them while we dance."

Lynn and Lydia looked at each other, then nodded their agreement to Maggie.

Following the two-hour class, they exited the studio and passed the Sacred Moon troupe. The members of both troupes greeted one another and exchanged hugs. Thanks to Maggie's gatherings and haflas, any jealousy had been replaced by friendship.

As the troupe progressed to Rhita's, Becca, Jewell and Lydia walked in a row together while Lynn joined Miranda and Z.

"Have you heard anything else from Elizabeth?" Becca asked.

"No, I think she's really out of our lives. I hope for good."

"I hope so too," Becca said.

"Me three," Lydia said.

"Whoa." Becca shook her head. "That was stressful."

"You're telling me. Caroline heard from Elizabeth's mother and she's back in England."

"Let's hope she finds some other unsuspecting man and lands him." Lydia placed three fingers over her mouth. "Did I say that?"

"It's not like she couldn't with those looks." Jewell paused. "As long as she doesn't speak and leak out any flames to reveal herself as a fire-breathing dragon."

Becca and Lydia laughed.

"Exactly." Becca drew the word out for emphasis.

Once in Rhita's with drinks purchased and seats claimed, the group buzzed with excitement for the upcoming Halloween party and planned to get together to practice.

Jewell lifted her white chocolate macadamia nut latte to her mouth and inhaled the sweet scent of nuts and chocolate. Her surroundings faded to the background for a few seconds as she savored the familiar sweetness. She recalled her first trip to Rhita's, and the memories filled her heart with love for these friends.

On the day of the party, Jewell and Christian climbed into the SUV with their pirate and tiny flamenco dancer. Once Olivia glimpsed her mother and grandmother's flamenco costumes, she wanted one for herself. Jewell and Candi had conspired to present Sophie and Olivia as the troupe's lucky charms.

Lydia and George planned to meet up with them and the troupe just outside the mansion.

Johnathan insisted on dressing in his costume the minute his feet hit the floor that morning.

"You might tire of it, buddy," Christian warned, but so far, he seemed thrilled to portray his favorite bandit.

He frequently pulled the plastic sword from its sheath and spread his feet in a wide stance. "Grab the loot, matey. I'll hold them off."

"Where'd he even get that?" Christian asked as he drove the outer perimeter seeking an open spot. Parking was slim as the town swelled with locals and visitors.

"When's Bitsy coming?" Johnathan asked.

"They're meeting us outside before we go in. With everyone else." Jewell watched her side of the street for an open spot. "Over there, Christian."

Once parked, Jewell lifted Olivia from her car seat and Christian lifted Johnathan to the ground, keeping hold of his hand. They retrieved Olivia's stroller from the back next to Romeo's carrier.

"Why didn't Romeo come?" Johnathan asked.

"Because they don't allow dogs inside the mansion." Jewell used her foot to open Olivia's stroller.

"But he's not a dog, he's Romeo."

Jewell and Christian chuckled. She secured Olivia in her stroller and arranged the clip-in red carnation in her dark curls, unsure how long it would stay there.

The sky was a bright blue with few clouds and it was warm for the first week in November, nearly 75 degrees. Jewell thought about ditching her lace shawl and kept watch on the kids for signs of overheating.

"I know!" Johnathan appeared deep in thought as the four traveled on foot toward the mansion. "Let's dress Romeo up for Halloween and then he can go in."

"Maybe next year."

"Hey, there's Bitsy. Can I run to her?"

"No, you cannot," Christian answered. "We'll be there soon enough."

"Look both ways, up and down the street," Jewell instructed. The traffic stopped, and they crossed to the side of the mansion. When they were close to Lydia and George, Christian let go of Johnathan's hand.

"Mom, you look great." Jewell admired Lydia in her costume with her glistening black hair pulled tightly in a bun. She was overjoyed to have Lydia dancing with the troupe.

"Yoo-hoo."

"I'd know that Southern accent anywhere." Jewell peered through the crowd. "Maggie is here somewhere."

Then she heard Z's piercing whistle.

"There's the gang," Christian said. He pointed to a spot in the lawn, just left of the mansion entrance. They were among a crowd of some fifty other visitors.

She saw Z bouncing up and down, waving wildly. Jewell chuckled to herself seeing her friend in makeup and a red carnation in her short hair.

"Aw, don't y'all just look like the perfect family," Maggie said.

"Are we all here?" Jewell scanned the crowd. "Hey, where are your folks meeting us, Christian?"

"Right around here." He peered through the crowd. "There they are. Stay here, I'll get them."

"Don't you look sweet," Maggie bent to Olivia's stroller while Becca fussed over Johnathan's costume. On cue, he pulled his sword from the sheath.

"Gabby took her dozen or so kids inside," Maggie said. "All dressed like some outer space fighter. Beats me what they are. We're still waiting for Sherry. Oh, and Candi went inside with Sophia and Tom. Just wait until you see Sophia."

Then she announced, "This is all of us."

"Wait, Christian is coming with Caroline and Roger."

Once they approached, the group proceeded in.

"I hope they let us in." Lynn progressed through the sea of people to stand next to Jewell in line as they waited to pay and enter. Her bright red carnation stood out on her slicked-back blonde hair. "Do you know what the capacity is?"

"Let's see," Jewell began. "I'd estimate each floor is around six thousand square feet, so times three floors gives us eighteen thousand square feet and for buildings of this nature, fire code runs around…hmmm, how many people per square feet?" Jewell glanced to the sky, mentally calculating as they waited in line to pay and check in. "Then, factor in the number of exits, an—"

Maggie twisted from ahead in line to interrupt. "It doesn't matter. We're dancing so they'll let us in." She cackled. "I'll see to it."

The crowd moved. Christian reached the cashier and purchased four tickets. Once they gathered inside, Maggie motioned to go upstairs. "Y'all," she shouted above the noise. "Let's go upstairs to the ballroom. We're on in forty-five minutes."

Jewell leaned her shoulder into Della Rae as they ascended the stairs. "Hey, Della Rae, look what I have tucked in here." Jewell wiggled her eyebrows, glancing down at her cleavage.

"Ooh la la, you naughty girl."

"Shh, I bought an extra red carnation and stuffed it here in honor of Lucia's stories. I don't know how long it will stay put between my A cups. Although, I'm almost a B now with the pregnancy!"

When they entered the ballroom, Jewell marveled over the festive feel. Pumpkins, lights and greenery tastefully decorated the room. She couldn't find a ghost or goblin anywhere in the trimmings. Her mouth watered at the sight of tables laden with refreshments lining the far wall. Her ears buzzed with the noise of the crowd and the music from a mariachi band playing in the background.

Jewell spotted Tyler, Tristan, Tabor and Teague slashing the air with neon swords. Soon, Gabby and Kevin approached.

"Hey, have you seen Candi and Tom?" Jewell asked.

"Yep, they're over there."

"Aw, c'mon, honey. I want to see Sophia and get some pics of her and Olivia together." Jewell pushed the stroller and checked to make sure Christian and Johnathan followed.

When it was time for their performance, the Historical Board President used a mic to encourage the guests to clear the middle of the floor and stand around the perimeter. He then made several announcements about the mansion and welcomed all who attended. He then nodded for the dancers to take their places. Once in formation, Maggie cued the DJ.

Familiar pre-performance butterflies overcame Jewell, but she took comfort in knowing her heroine, Aniela, felt the same apprehension before a show. She took deep breaths and launched into the moves. When they finished dancing, the crowd roared.

"That was great, babe," Christian rushed with the kids to greet her.

"Yeah, and Bitsy too," Johnathan said.

They filled their plates with snacks and sweets from the buffet table. Jewell admired people's creativity as she tried to take in every unique costume.

With plates in hand, filled from a second round, Jewell and Christian stood with Lydia and George.

"Lydia," George said. "There's Dr. Herrera with her family. Would you like to meet her before your appointment on Tuesday?"

"Appointment!" Jewell snapped. "What appointment?"

"Oh, dear." Lydia tugged at the scarf around her neck. "It's just a checkup. I haven't established my care with anyone here."

"Is everything okay, Mom?"

"Of course it is." Lydia took a bite. "These crab balls are amazing." Jewell eyed her.

"Okay, George. Let's go meet her. Are you coming, Jewell?"

"No, that's okay. But do you want me to go to your appointment with you?"

"Heavens no. I'll be fine."

Jewell glanced down at Olivia to see her covered in chocolate cupcake and orange icing. She nudged for Christian to look.

"Oops, I think it's time this family unit headed home."

Jewell did her best to clean up the icing mess on Olivia. Johnathan tugged on Christian's pant leg. When he stooped, Johnathan whispered in his ear.

Christian stood. "Seems we need to visit the little boy's room on the way out."

They stopped on the bottom floor and Jewell wheeled Olivia around the lobby, seeing it with fresh eyes.

"Lola." Jewell heard a familiar voice approaching from behind.

"What?" She turned, puzzled. It was Kage. She pinched her eyebrows together. "Huh?"

"Your costume."

"Oh." She shook her head. "No, I'm Floriana Lucia Ramos y Montoya."

"Whatever you say. But…Jewell?" Kage nodded toward Olivia. "I'm trying to do the math here."

"Relax!" Jewell peeked around the stroller to see Olivia napping.

"She's Nathanael's."

"Really?" Kage scanned the place.

"No, don't look for him he's n—"

"There you are." A considerably pregnant Anna appeared at Kage's side.

Jewell's eyes darted to the young woman's rounded middle just as Christian and Johnathan arrived.

"Hello," Christian greeted the couple standing with his wife and daughter.

"Christian, this is Kage"—she watched her husband's eyes widen—"and Anna."

"Nice to meet you both." Christian shook their hands.

"And this is our son, Johnathan." Jewell chuckled inside at Kage's expression, figuring he was trying to do the math again.

Jewell felt hands on her shoulders. She turned, and it was Liz with her bright white teeth.

"Hi, sweetheart," Liz greeted.

Jewell turned to hug her.

"Great to see you all," Jewell said. "We have two kids to get home. Congratulations on your growing family."

"Isn't it the greatest?" Liz jumped in before anyone else answered.

"Yes it is," Jewell agreed. "We'll see you all later."

As Jewell exited the mansion with her family, she looked back at the building and whispered...

"Where did you disappear to, Lucia?"

Eleven

Epilogue

J ewell stood at the counter attempting to follow Lydia's recipe for Chicken Marsala for dinner that night. She figured she'd better get the hang of cooking for her family since Lydia was spending more and more time at George's house. Jewell braced herself each day expecting Lydia's inevitable announcement she was moving in with George.

She heard the door open. Lydia was home from yet a second doctor's appointment.

"What is it, Mom? You look pale."

"Let's go to the dining room."

Jewell dropped her hands into the chicken and stared.

"Bitsy is home." Johnathan rushed to Lydia with Olivia toddling behind.

"Hey, sweetpeas," Lydia said. "Bitsy needs to talk to Mommy a minute. Then I'll be right back."

Jewell jiggled her hands over the chicken, then washed them. She carried the dish towel with her to the dining room, still drying her hands. Lydia had already pulled two chairs out, seated in one.

"What is it?"

"Dr. Herrera discussed some test results today."

"Yes?" Jewell felt the blood rush from her face.

"My cancer is back."

About the Author

Hi, I'm Cathryn Petit and I hope you are enjoying the tales of Jewell and her friends as they journey through life. As a bellydancer myself, I understand the threads of friendship that bond dancers as they share this art form.

Reviews are crucial for any author, and even just one line or two can make a vast difference. I would appreciate a review on Amazon. In addition, your review can help other readers pick up this book and enjoy Jewell's adventures.

Thank you in advance.

Please keep reading to learn about the other books in the series! Also, follow me on any of the links ahead for updates on the launch of the series' audiobooks narrated by the talented Angela Petry!

Connect with me:

You can connect with me on:

🌐 https://www.cathrynlynnpetit.com

◼ https://bit.ly/2VakFF8

Subscribe to my newsletter:

✉ https://www.cathrynlynnpetit.com/contact

Also by Cathryn Petit

YOUR FAVORITE SISTERS ARE GROWING! THE SISTERS OF THE SILK VEIL SERIES NOW COMPRISES THREE FULL BOOKS AND A SHORT-STORY PREQUEL. (Please bear with me as the series covers go through a transformation.)

Book 1: Sisters of the Silk Veil: A Troupe Emerges
A story of Longing, adventure, tragedy and an ultimate rebirth...

Torn between caring for her boyfriend who's crippled with phobias or breaking away to the life of her dreams, JEWELL CALDWELL, a beautiful young genius, contrives a plan to ease Josh's agoraphobia so she can move cross country to find the life of her dreams.

In the quaint Florida town she moves to, she stumbles into a bellydance studio and makes fast friends with the dancers.

When a handsome rancher struts into her life, she sees the chance for happiness beyond her wildest imagination. But, tragedy strikes, and Jewell fears she is the cause. Plagued by a blackmailer, guilt and grief, she plunges into despair and isolation.

Will she learn to truly open up to others in order to regain her happiness or plod through life desperate and alone?

Lydia: A Sisters of the Silk Veil Series Prequel
Learn about the events leading to Jewell's turbulent childhood...

The story of Lydia is empathetic and claustrophobic giving a stark insight into how easy it is to fall into a negative spiral. We follow Lydia as she struggles to look after her young family as the institutional and bureaucratic nets close evermore tightly around her.

Book 2: A Spell of Wanderlust
Wanderlust, a mystery woman and murder...

Struck by a spell of wanderlust when a professional bellydancer visits the Silk Veil Studio, JEWELL CALDWELL plots the journey of her lifetime and turns her Southbridge world upside down.

The exploration includes intriguing locations across the nation with plans to learn from bellydance instructors who possess unique specialties. Her first stop—Southern California—where the inspiring visitor to Maggie's studio, ANIELA, resides and teaches.

There, she explores the area and meets other dancers, including the handsome ANDREA whose performance melts her.

The visit exceeds Jewell's expectations until a health crisis and a stranger shake her world. As she's recovering, she receives an urgent call to return to Southbridge. A troupe member is in hot water and the group finds it necessary to take matters into their own hands to solve the crime and clear her name.

Follow Jewell on yet another journey where she learns the meaning of forgiveness and true love.